PERFECT SHELTER

Deborah Pierson Dill

PERFECT SHELTER

Publishing History
First White Rose Edition, 2010
Print Edition ISBN 978-1-61116-011-6
Published in the United States of America

Prologue

Blithe Settlement, Texas
Spring 2004

"*Please*, God!"

Elaine stopped pounding and straining against the storm cellar door and held her breath, listening for some sign of help. A mockingbird chirped and sang happily, as if nothing had happened. A dog barked somewhere in the distance. Aside from that nothing. No sound. What if no one ever came?

Don't be stupid. She shook her head to dislodge the unnerving prospect. *Of course someone will come.* Too late! Fear clamped like a vise around her heart. She raised a hand to clutch at her tightening chest. If only there was a little light down here, it wouldn't be so bad. Up until now she'd done all right. But each minute that passed, each futile shove against the obstructed door, made it harder to contain the panic rising from the pit of her stomach trying to claw its way out.

She had to get out of here! But she could barely breathe, let alone move whatever had landed on top of the door. What if it was her truck or one of Mr. Chandler's Longhorns? She pushed again, measuring the result this time. No. It wasn't that solid. But it wasn't moving either. She bent forward and braced her hands on her knees, gasping desperately to fill constricted lungs.

Don't scream. She took a deep breath. *It won't help.* She let it out. *No one will hear.* She stood up straight again, her head throbbing in time with the rhythm of her pounding pulse. The Chandlers, her nearest neighbors, lived a mile down the road. They had been a great source of help and comfort to her since Richard's death. The tightness in her chest bore down again, nearly driving her to her knees. But she'd run for the storm cellar without thinking to grab her phone. She had no way to contact them or anyone. She'd have to figure a way out of this alone. She closed her eyes and breathed.

"Please, God."

This time the words sounded calmer, less desperate, ready to negotiate as if God didn't know exactly how hopeless she was.

The sound of rustling debris nearly stopped her heart.

Her eyes snapped open, then she froze. *Surely not.* Surely she had not locked herself down here with something alive. She held her breath. Maybe she'd just imagined it. But the sound came again. Something moved. Or had it slithered? She spun around, slammed her open palms against the door and pushed with an adrenaline fed strength she didn't possess under ordinary circumstances. The obstruction outside shifted. Whatever had her trapped down here scraped and slid against the door. She shoved again and it lifted slightly, a couple of inches.

"Yes!"

She took a deep, determined breath, then wiped away tears she hadn't, until just now, realized had fallen. She braced herself, and shoved again. The sound of splintering wood on the outside was like music to her ears. She kept pushing, and her captor kept giving way. Daylight! *Thank you, God!*

She could only raise the door a foot or so. But that was all the space she needed. She pushed and pulled and squirmed her way back above ground. When she finally emerged into the gray afternoon light she sank to her knees, trembling and gasping for breath. *Thank you, God!*

For a long moment she knelt there, filling her lungs with fresh, cool air. Her pulse slowed, and the tightness in her chest relaxed. She swallowed repeatedly, trying to ease the soreness in her parched throat.

Water. That's what she needed. After a long cool drink she'd assess the damage. She pushed herself up off the rain soaked grass and turned for the house, but stopped short at the sight before her. The tightness in her chest returned and stole her breath as effectively as a punch to the gut. A pile of battered lumber and spewing broken plumbing lay where her beautiful home had stood not more than twenty minutes ago. Nothing remained intact except a border of immaculate, untouched flower beds filled with pink snapdragons.

Tears surged. She sniffed and tried to blink them away. Then she tried to rub them away. She turned back to the storm cellar. There *had* been a tornado. She *had* been down in the shelter. The tree that had been uprooted and tossed on top of the doors still lay there blocking the entrance. The lacerations and abrasions all over her arms, face and back from pushing her way out were real, stinging, and bleeding. She turned around again. The house was still gone.

God, what now? It was all she could do to keep from falling back to her knees and shouting the question straight to heaven. *First Richard's death, now this?*

Had it really only been four weeks? She squeezed her eyes shut against the coming memory.

"Elaine, there's been an accident." Justin Barnet had broken the news.

An accident… The word echoed in her mind.

In her mind's eye Elaine pushed the screen door open and stepped onto her front porch, sheltered from the full force of the thunderstorm but still feeling the spray of it on her face.

"It's Richard," Justin continued, tears filling his eyes. "Elaine, he's…"

"What's going on?" Panic flared hot and bright. Elaine turned to the sheriff, Ed Lacey, who stood beside Justin. "What's happened?"

"Elaine, the creek is just running so high and fast. The current must have knocked his feet out from under him."

"Where is he?" Elaine dashed back into the house and grabbed a raincoat off the rack by the door, then pulled it on as she pushed her way back out the door.

"At the hospital, but Elaine—"

She nodded. "OK. What's wrong? How is he?"

Justin stopped her with a hand on her shoulder. "Elaine, he's gone."

She felt something like a punch in the stomach. It took the wind right out of her. "He…he's…what?"

"He drowned."

Elaine remembered feeling her knees buckle and Justin catching her before she hit the porch, but could recall nothing else about that day except the sight of Richard's body, cold and lifeless on the hospital gurney.

Now the home they'd shared was gone, too.

God, what will You take next? What do I have left? Aunt Laura?

Aunt Laura! She should get to town, to check on her great aunt. She should check on her neighbors. Together they'd come up with a plan. Somebody had to have a plan. She turned and ran for the driveway, but stopped dead after a few strides. Her truck...She scanned the rubble and the pasture beyond, but it was nowhere in sight. And that could only mean that, wherever it had landed, it probably wasn't fit to drive.

Something hung from a limb of a mangled mesquite tree across the field. She squinted hard, trying to bring it into focus through her tear-blurred vision. Her purse? Elaine rushed for it, stirring a small flock of screeching guineas from their refuge in a patch of tall buffalo grass.

A spark of anger flashed inside her. "How is it," she muttered to the sky, wiping her running nose on the cuff of her sleeve, "that those stupid birds survived, but my home—*my life!*—is gone? Haven't I tried to please You? Haven't I done everything I was supposed to do?"

The spark set fire to something inside and it drove her. She clambered up into the tree to find her purse still zipped and, except for hanging from a tree limb, perfectly normal. Not a scratch on it. She dropped back to the ground and pulled open the zipper. Everything was there; cash, credit cards, lip gloss, keys.

"Thank You *so* much for sparing my keys!" With a furious shout she drew her arm back and threw the keys as hard as she could toward the rubble.

The sound of a siren drifted intermittently through the silence, growing steadier and louder as the gray clouds began to break up and give way to clear blue patches of sky. A cool breeze picked up, as if what had preceded it had been the gentlest of showers. It would be a perfect spring day—at least what was left of it would be. The irony brought a fresh sting of tears.

She *should* be thankful for her life. Elaine cast another glance at the scattered debris. If she hadn't been caught outside...If she'd gone to the house instead of that musty old cellar...She'd be dead.

But no. She wouldn't thank God for sparing her life. Why should she? What good was her life after everything He'd taken from her? What kind of pawn was she in His perfect *plan*? And what kind of plan was it that stripped her of everything truly important and left her with nothing but a useless set of keys? She was finished with trying to please God. She turned from the scene, slung her purse over her shoulder, and started walking.

A sheriff's department patrol car rolled slowly down the debris strewn road toward her as she climbed over a tree that had dropped like a twig, blocking its progress. Almost before the car had come to a stop, the driver's door flew open. Justin Barnet jumped out and ran toward her.

She gritted her teeth and suppressed a groan. This was the last thing she needed. Sweet, solicitous Justin, telling her that everything would be OK was the absolute *last* thing in the world she needed at this moment.

"Elaine, are you OK? Are you hurt?"

"I'm fine."

"You're not fine." Justin surveyed her from head to toe, then he reached out to her, as if to offer support. "You're bleeding. Elaine...your house..."

She shrugged away from his touch and fought hard to resist the impulse to physically push him away. "It's gone." Her voice trembled with rage, but she was so tired of pretending to be OK she made no effort to mask it.

Justin glanced from the remains of her home and back to her again, the stunned look on his face expressing plainly that he had never before witnessed this level of destruction either.

Elaine followed his gaze back to the rubble. "Can you give me a ride into town?"

಼ಾ಼ಾ

"Elaine, the bus is here."

Elaine started and tore her gaze away from the television set behind the convenience store counter. How long had she been here, staring at the Weather Channel? She glanced at her watch. Almost two hours.

"Elaine, darlin'? Did you hear me?"

She nodded, stood, and stretched. "Yes. Thank you, Mrs. Simon. I'm ready."

When she turned for the door, she almost ran right into Justin.

"I was hoping I'd make it before the bus got here."

For a second the breath caught in her chest and she couldn't tear her gaze from his. His eyes always looked so startlingly blue, but they seemed particularly intense just now. Maybe it was the way they contrasted with his dark hair and lashes. Or maybe it was something about the tan of his uniform. Maybe it was the now cloudless blue sky visible through the clear glass door behind him. Maybe she could get lost in those eyes and forget everything that had happened up until this moment. He loved her. That was something she still had.

"Where are you gonna go?" The sound of his voice drew her unwillingly back to reality.

Elaine shrugged, looking down to fidget with the ticket in her hand. "The bus is going to Dallas."

He swallowed. "What's in Dallas?"

"Guess I'll find out when I get there." She tried to smile. "I have a few friends…"

"You have friends here." Justin's voice sounded hoarse. "Stay."

She shook her head and pinched the bridge of her nose to stem the coming flow of tears. "I don't want to stay here." She forced the words past her constricted throat. "I don't want to live here anymore. I never wanted to come back here, anyway…" She let her voice trail off with another shake of head. "I'm gonna find another place." She took a deep breath and made up her mind for good, steeling herself against the look of desolation on Justin's face. "Maybe in Dallas, maybe somewhere else entirely. But not here. I just can't stay here anymore."

"Elaine…" He took a few steps toward her. "I know you've had a bad time these last few weeks…" He stopped and shook his head as if he knew the words were totally insufficient. "Since Richard…" His voice broke and he drew in a deep shuddering breath, dropping his gaze to his boots. "You've got friends here, too. There are people who love you here. What about your aunt and everybody at church. They'll take care of you." He met her gaze again. "I'll take care of you. God will take care of you."

"You think?" Even when he dropped his gaze to the floor, she didn't regret the bitter sentiment. But she did regret directing it at him. She laid an apologetic hand on his arm, then started to move past him, but he took hold of her hand and turned her to face him.

"Elaine, don't go." Before she could pull herself free, he drew her close and wrapped his arms around her. "Please don't go," he whispered against her hair.

She stiffened and raised her hands to his chest to push him away, but as he held her tightly all the fight drained out of her. Her eyelids drifted closed and she breathed deeply, finally leaning into him, letting him hold her. Her arms slid around him and she laid her head against his shoulder, feeling comfort for the first time since Richard's death.

Oh, Justin. She nearly sighed his name. Maybe she could stay. Maybe she should. Justin *would* take care of her, even if she never loved him the way she'd loved Richard...

Richard. No. She shook her head and pushed away from him.

Justin might take care of her, but she had her doubts as to whether God would. And she would not stay here, the place to which He had so clearly called her and Richard, and subject herself to more heartache at the hands of a God whom she had spent her life trying to please.

"I won't stay here." She took a big step back, shaking her head. Then she turned and walked quickly away from him. Tears threatened, and she couldn't let them get the better of her again. If she started crying now, she feared she'd never stop.

Outside the bus waited. She climbed aboard, fighting the impulse to look back. Knowing that if she did, she might regret leaving, and leaving was something she needed to do now. She squeezed her eyes shut and breathed deeply. But as the bus lurched forward Justin's name drifted through her mind and she turned to look out the window despite her intention not to.

Justin stood, hands on his hips, head hung in dejection. Glancing up as the bus turned to leave the parking lot, he noticed her watching him. He took one step, then another toward the bus. Elaine pressed her palm to the window in farewell then turned away as the bus pulled onto the highway.

1

Blithe Settlement, Texas
Five years later

"Aunt Laura?"

The screen door closed with a creak behind her as Elaine stepped tentatively in among the golden oak paneled walls of her great aunt's living room. Chilly air from outside had come in by way of the wide open front door. No telling how long it had been open. She pushed it closed, and set her purse and suitcase on the floor next to the staircase.

"Hello?" The television was on with the volume turned up as loud as it would go. "Aunt Laura?" She retrieved the remote from an end table and turned the sound down. The whir of an electric mixer came from the direction of the kitchen.

She shed her jacket and hung it on the coat rack, then turned and surveyed the room. She might as well have stepped back in time twenty years. The Christmas tree, with fat twinkle bulbs, crocheted snowflakes, and angels, stood grandly in its traditional place next to the staircase. An evergreen garland spiraled around the banister. A crackling fire burned in the fireplace, already overcoming the chill that had settled in the room.

She sucked in a breath and held it, steeling herself

11

against the warm fuzzy nostalgia. She wasn't coming home. This visit would only last a few days. She'd check on her aunt, make sure everything was OK here, then she'd go. Lately this place; the town, her old friends, her home all seemed to draw her back as the details surrounding her departure grew hazy and indistinct. Her motivation for leaving faded a little from her memory with each passing day. But Blithe Settlement was still the last place she ever wanted to be.

The sound of the mixer stopped.

"Aunt Laura?" She stepped toward the kitchen.

"Elaine, honey, is that you?"

"In the flesh." Elaine found her aunt standing over the kitchen counter in a pink terry cloth bathrobe, quickly dropping spoonfuls of divinity onto a sheet of wax paper. Her silky, fine hair had gone completely white since Elaine had been away, but her fair skin was still smooth and soft looking.

Finished, Laura put the mixer bowl into the sink and turned to Elaine.

"Let me look at you!" She outstretched her arms for a thorough hug and then stepped back again. "You've gotten taller."

"No." Elaine grinned.

"You've gotten thinner?"

"Maybe a little."

Laura stepped back and examined her with a critical eye.

"You've cut your hair!" she said. "And had your eyebrows waxed! Oh, good for you. It was unfortunate that you inherited the Maitland brow. I'm sorry for that."

"Well, it wasn't your fault," Elaine said with a

smirk.

"No, it was your grandmother's. Did you just get here?"

Elaine nodded.

"Oh, did you close the front door?"

Elaine nodded again. "Mm hm. I also turned the T.V. down a little."

"Was the movie over yet?" Laura furrowed her brow. "When it's over it's time for me to start getting ready."

"Well, I don't think it was, but halfway or so." Elaine leaned over the counter. Divinity was a family Christmas tradition. Her mouth watered at the prospect of sneaking a piece while it was still soft and warm. "You know, you *could* put a clock in here. Or get a new microwave. They have clocks built right in now."

Laura gave her a glance that blatantly accused her of being too big for her britches. "My life's too close to finished to start messing with clocks, honey. Or new microwaves, for that matter. And that old one works just fine. Oh, go ahead and have a piece." She pointed a rubber spatula at the setting divinity.

Elaine took a piece of the soft, warm candy and bit into it, barely suppressing a blissful groan and letting her eyes roll heavenward at the taste. "What do you have to get ready for?"

"We're having a Christmas party tonight at six o'clock."

Elaine choked. "We are? Tonight? At six?"

"Yes, did you bring something nice to wear?"

"Uh...I, uh...Depends on what you mean by nice."

"A Christmas party dress, honey." Laura began scrubbing the dishes in the sink.

"I didn't bring anything really nice. I guess I didn't plan on going to any fancy parties while I was here."

"Don't worry about it." Laura dismissed the error with a wave of her soapy dishrag. "I picked you out something from downtown. Just in case."

"Aunt Laura, you didn't have to—"

"It's just a little pre-Christmas gift." Laura shot her a coy glance. "Besides you're the guest of honor. You have to look special."

Elaine grinned. Something made of gold lamé, no doubt. Or covered with sequins. Or possibly both. Then Laura's words caught up with her.

"Guest of honor?"

"Yes, honey." Laura sounded as if she thought Elaine had gone stupid. "Now go take a bath."

~∂∙∂~

Elaine examined her reflection in the full length mirror in her room. The outfit *was* a little on the sparkly side. And the shoes…She'd never owned a pair of shoes with such pointy little toes. Another item that Laura had thought to include was a clip for her hair. Elaine picked it up off the dresser and ran a finger over the shiny gold and silver beads. She raised her free hand and smoothed the short fringe at the nape of her neck. She had loved her long hair when she'd been younger. Richard had adored it. She couldn't remember what had prompted her to have it cut. But she *could* remember how she'd nearly burst into tears right there in the beauty salon at the sight of her long, dark tresses scattered on the floor.

She smoothed a lock behind one ear and sighed. In this mirror she could see so clearly how the years had changed her. Her complexion was pale, her grey eyes dull, and she looked older. She ran a hand lightly across the skin of her cheek. No, she wasn't as pretty as she'd once been. But she was stronger. The thought gave her a small measure of satisfaction.

The doorbell rang and she dropped the hair clip back onto the dresser, half-heartedly fluffing her hair once more before heading to the staircase to join the party. Already the voices of old friends drifted up the stairs and through the hall, underscored by soft instrumental Christmas music. *The Holly and the Ivy.*

And that was Ed Lacey's robust, twangy voice greeting Aunt Laura now. Elaine felt a smile soften her features as she reached the top of the stairs and saw him standing there next to his wife, Dot, both of them completely unchanged.

Ed looked up and caught sight of her. His open stare was curious at first, but then recognition lit his features and he bounded halfway up the staircase to greet her with a tight hug and a big grin. He squeezed a little laugh out of her, and it was only his burly arms that kept her from losing her footing and tumbling the rest of the way down the stairs.

"Elaine!" He looked her up and down as if he couldn't quite believe his eyes. "Elaine! Darlin' it's so good to see you. Where have you been?"

"Um...San Antonio mostly."

"We've missed you, girl." Ed's voice was tender. Almost as tender as it had been the day he and Justin had come to her door to tell her that her husband was dead.

"I've missed y'all, too." She looked away, swallowing down the ache that began to form at the back of her throat. *Do not cry! No one here wants to see*

15

your tears after all these years.

"Well, you're home now." Ed took her by the arm and whisked her down the stairs to greet Dot. "It was mighty sneaky of your Aunt not to tell anyone that you'd be back in town this Christmas."

Elaine shot a quick glance at Laura, who was hanging up her guests' coats, a sly smile lighting her features. "Yes, it was."

A gasp from the living room caught her attention. "It's Elaine!"

Guests already assembled in front of the crackling fire turned and parted, drawing her into their midst, greeting her with the same delight as Ed and Dot had a moment before. Elaine met them all with hugs and handshakes, smiling stiffly at first, totally overwhelmed. Torn between her need to remain detached to ensure an easy departure in four days' time, and this crazy, sudden urge to burst into tears and admit just how good it felt to be home again.

She was not coming home. The thought came to her again, as it had just a few hours ago. But she felt her heart soften just a little, anyway. What could it hurt? For one night, what could it hurt to be glad she'd come back? And enjoy catching up with these who, it seemed a lifetime ago, had been friends, congregation members, and co-workers of Richard's and hers?

Somehow over the din of the small crowd around her, Elaine heard another gasp, then: "Elaine Mallory!"

She turned to locate the source of the cry, and found Lorraine Barnet standing beside the twinkling Christmas tree, eyes wide, arms outstretched, and a cane in one hand. Elaine went to her.

"Oh, honey! I never thought I'd see you again." Mrs. Barnet embraced her then took a step back. "Let me look at you!"

Elaine couldn't suppress her smile now if she tried. She did a slow spin, letting Mrs. Barnet look her over. When she came back around she found herself staring straight over Mrs. Barnet's shoulder and into Justin Barnet's blue eyes.

She righted herself and fought the initial impulse to take a few steps backward. In the five years she'd been gone, nothing had ever brought the memory of that spring back to her like the sight of those eyes did at this moment. Richard's death, the memory of his cold, ashen body on the stretcher, the sight of the rubble to which her whole life had been reduced; all of it came rushing back just like the flood waters that had started it.

But it was Justin, her oldest friend. Her eyes went a little misty and the corners of her mouth began to curve into a smile. Despite the memories swirling around him, it was good to see him again.

"Justin." She took a step toward him, but he didn't reciprocate.

"Elaine." His tone didn't match the warmth of hers. She felt her smile fade a little, though she tried to cover it.

"Justin, I'm so glad you could come." Aunt Laura took Mrs. Barnet's coat, then turned for Justin's.

"I can't stay." He took a step backward toward the door.

"Oh, please stay!" Aunt Laura cajoled.

"No." He held up a hand. "Thank you, Miss Laura, I can't. I have something I need to do."

Mrs. Barnet's brows drew together. "What, honey?"

"Christine Mosely called about a half hour ago.

One of her boys sent a baseball through the living room window. She asked if I could fix it for her tomorrow. But I need to at least board it up tonight."

"But you'll come when you're finished?" Mrs. Barnet asked. "Elaine's here! You two should catch up."

Justin glanced back at Elaine and she offered him another smile, though this one felt a little forced. He cast his gaze to the floor. "I'll be back to drive you home later," he said to his mother. "If you're ready to leave before I get here, just give me a call."

He shot one more glance at Elaine, then turned and walked out.

∂∞∽

"Go ahead and ask, honey. I know you want to." Aunt Laura's whispered lure might have worked to pique her interest if it hadn't already been so aroused.

Elaine stacked her load of dishes in the sink next to Laura's. The party was winding down and most of the guests had already gone home, leaving only Ed and Dot, and Lorraine Barnet still sitting a little awkwardly by the fire.

"Ask what?" Elaine whispered back.

"Why Justin didn't stay."

"He had a favor to do for Christine Mosely."

Aunt Laura gave Elaine an assessing look, one eyebrow rising slowly. Probably in response to the slightly snide way she'd drawled Christine's name. Then Aunt Laura slowly shook her head.

"OK. Why didn't he stay?"

"Shh." Laura put a finger to her lips and peeked around the corner into the living room. "I'll tell you later. I can't leave Lorraine in there alone with them for too long. It gets uncomfortable for her."

"Aunt Laura!"

But it was too late, Laura had already swished out of the room in her Christmas-red taffeta party dress and was on her way back to her guests. Elaine was left completely unsatisfied and thoroughly intrigued by the lingering question she hadn't even brought up. She turned and followed Laura to the living room where Ed and Dot were putting on their coats.

"You're not leaving so soon!" Laura objected as Ed put his camel colored cowboy hat on and handed Dot her purse.

"Well, I think I just heard Justin pull up out front." He confided to Laura quietly. Then he turned to Elaine with a point of his finger. "Don't you be a stranger, young lady."

She smiled. "I'll do my best."

Ed and Dot slipped out the front door and into the chilly December night. Elaine crossed the room to the front window, pulled back the curtain, and watched them go. Ed had been right, it was Justin. The two men passed each other on the front lawn with not a word spoken between them. They didn't even look at each other. *What's up with that?*

Elaine chanced a glance back at Mrs. Barnet who returned a sad gaze. She ought to march right across this room and just ask what had gone so wrong between Justin and Ed. The two men had been good friends. Ed had been Justin's mentor at the Sheriff's Department. They used to take fishing trips together. But before she could act on the impulse Justin came through the front door which Laura had been holding open.

"You ready, Mama?"

Elaine glanced down, embarrassed by the abrupt way he spoke to his mother.

"Well, no," Lorraine said softly. "I'd really like to stay a bit longer. Why don't you come and sit with us for awhile?"

"Yes! Why don't you? I'll make you a cup of coffee, or would you prefer cider? Here give me your coat."

When Elaine raised her gaze again, she found Laura had descended like an avalanche and taken him over so quickly that he shrugged his shoulders out of his coat while she peeled it from his arms, all before he had a chance to protest.

"Um...coffee, thanks." His manner eased only slightly as his glance traveled from his mother, to Laura who was hanging up his coat, and then to her. And then to the curtain she still clutched in her hand.

She let the panel go and clasped both hands behind her back. "Merry Christmas, Justin," she said softly. His gaze met hers.

"Merry Christmas to you, too, Elaine." All traces of his former gruffness vanished when he said her name. "It's been a long time."

"Oh, not so long," she said absently, recalling the images that had overwhelmed her when she'd seen him earlier.

"Longer than you think."

She crossed to a chair and clutched the back with both hands, unable to tear her gaze away from his pained expression. This was not the Justin she remembered.

"Well." Aunt Laura's bright voice broke the melancholy mood that had suddenly engulfed them.

"I'll get your coffee. Be right back."

Justin sat down on the hearth with the crackling fire at his back and leaned forward, elbows on knees, and hands clasped in front of him, watching as Laura disappeared into the kitchen.

"So." His voice sounded deeper, richer, older, and Elaine could feel his gaze follow her as she crossed the room to take a seat in an old wingback chair. "Did y'all have a good party?"

When she looked back up at Justin, he looked toward his mother. "I bet Elaine here was a big surprise," he continued, glancing down at his clasped hands. "I don't guess anyone ever expected to see you again."

Elaine cleared her throat. "Everyone seemed quite surprised."

"It was a nice party, Justin," Mrs. Barnet said softly. "It's too bad you couldn't have stayed for it." She turned her focus to Elaine and smiled. "Justin's always so helpful. Like tonight, bringin' me here since Vic is out of town. I don't suppose you'd heard I'm getting remarried?"

Elaine shook her head and continued to listen politely as Mrs. Barnet went on, first about wedding plans and then about the arthritis that had taken its painful toll. But frequently during the soft-spoken monologue Elaine would glance back over at Justin, and would sometimes find him watching her.

She didn't even notice Aunt Laura had come back into the room until she offered Justin a steaming mug of coffee. He thanked her quietly, wrapping both hands around the hot cup and bringing it carefully to his lips for a taste. His dark hair was longer than he used to keep it. Elaine tilted her head and felt a soft smile touch her lips. He'd go to the barber's shop at least once a month for a cut so short he nearly looked military, insisting it was part of the deputy sheriff's uniform.

Aunt Laura's boisterous laugh startled her, and she glanced around, hoping no one had noticed her wandering attention. But when her gaze focused again on Justin, everything else blurred into the background.

The hair wasn't the only difference. She remembered him for many things, not the least of which was that he had been a happy man. His feelings for her had always been apparent. Indeed, his feelings about anything had always been painfully conspicuous. As a boy in school he had no shame at all about showing how much he liked her. Even as a grown man his affection for her had been obvious. And his loyalty had never faltered.

Even when she'd found happiness in marriage to another man, his friendship had remained steadfast. Elaine looked down at her knees as a heated rush of regret surfaced. She had always taken Justin's regard for her for granted, and when she married, she still expected no less from him. And he had delivered. He had befriended Richard wholeheartedly.

But this man...Elaine glanced back up at him. This man, sitting across the room from her now, closed and joyless, was not Justin.

He cast a quick glance at her and she turned away. Heat flooded her face. He must be making a similar assessment; wondering at her thinness, her paleness, her strained smile. She, too, had changed, and not necessarily for the better. But she had come back stronger and more self-reliant. If she'd proven nothing else by leaving here, she'd proven that she could take care of herself. She was in complete control.

Aunt Laura shifted in her seat on the sofa, leaning forward to collect some more dishes. Elaine sprang to her feet.

"Aunt Laura, let me do that." She quickly stacked the dishes with efficiency born of seemingly endless shifts waiting tables. Without pausing to hear her aunt's protests, she carried them to the kitchen. Setting them gently into the sink, she braced both hands on the cool tile of the counter. She squeezed her eyes shut against the sudden memory of Justin's devastated expression as the bus to Dallas had merged onto the highway the day she left. It was no wonder he didn't seem pleased to see her.

Heavy footsteps coming her way on the wood floor spurred her back to life. Justin set his empty mug on the counter beside the sink as Elaine started the tap running so the dishes could soak. He stood there beside her for a long moment, like he wanted to talk but didn't know exactly where to begin. Well, neither did she. But the silence was beginning to unnerve her, so she asked what she'd wanted to know all evening.

"So, are you and Christine...?"

He shook his head. "Her husband ran off and left her."

Elaine nodded. "I remember."

"I just try to help out where I can."

"Is Ed keeping you pretty busy?" Obviously things weren't right between him and Ed. She probably shouldn't ask about his work. More than likely it wouldn't soften his disposition. But what difference could that possibly make now?

"I don't work for the Sheriff's Department anymore."

Elaine blinked and closed her mouth, feeling her brows knit together. He loved that job. Why would he quit? But it didn't concern her, and she wouldn't be here for more than a few days anyway. Best not to reconnect with him too much. "Sorry," she mumbled. "I didn't know."

He set his mug in the sink. "Well, I'm gonna take Mama home. It was good seeing you."

"Um...yeah. You, too."

"If I don't see you again before you leave," Justin said with a finality that brought a sudden irritating lump to her throat, "take care of yourself."

He turned back to the living room. Elaine turned off the water and followed him. Laura had already helped Lorraine on with her coat and the two women stood at the front door awaiting Justin's return.

He turned and directed one last smile at her. But Elaine saw something altogether different in his eyes. She swallowed hard, suddenly hearing the words he'd said to her on the day she left town, as clearly as if he had just now said them.

Don't go, he had entreated softly against her ear. She could almost still feel his breath against her cheek and his warm, strong arms around her. Those words were a far cry from the *take care of yourself* he had muttered to her just a few seconds ago.

2

"Aunt Laura, what's in this box?"

Elaine dragged a chair into her bedroom closet to make a closer inspection of a large box up on the top shelf with her name written on the side in bold black letters. She pulled out an old water-stained high school yearbook, then she took the whole box down and moved it to the bed.

"What box, honey?" Laura came into the room carrying some blankets and an extra pillow.

"This box." She picked up the yearbook again. "I found it in the closet."

"Oh, that." Laura crossed to stand beside her. "For awhile after the tornado, folks out near where you lived would find things in odd places. They mostly just returned what they found to who they thought it belonged to. All your things got taken to the church."

Laura picked up a refrigerator magnet with Elaine's name painted on it. It had been a gift from the little girls' Sunday school class her first Christmas here with Richard.

Elaine furrowed her brow. "So, other buildings were damaged besides the parsonage?"

"Well, yes." Laura tapped a finger on her chin. "The Church was pretty torn up, though not totally demolished like your house. Needed a whole new roof, and all those stained glass windows." She gave a regretful *tsk* and shook her head. "Such a shame.

"Then there was the Chandlers' place. Oh, they just built a new house to replace their old one. And the Younts. They didn't lose everything, but they had some cleaning up to do."

"Huh." The incredulous response slipped out before she could stop it.

"Well, honey, you didn't think God had singled you out, did you?"

If she didn't know better she'd suspect sarcasm lay just beneath the surface of her aunt's comment. *Well, yes.* She wanted to say. *As a matter of fact, I did.* But the more the idea bounced around in her head, the sillier it sounded.

"Anyway," Aunt Laura continued, "after a year or so everyone figured you probably wouldn't be back, so they asked if I'd see that you got these things."

"People just found all this stuff layin' around?" She sat down on the bed and dug one hand into the box closing her eyes, trying to determine what each object was by its feel. Her hand found something cold and smooth. She grabbed it and pulled it from underneath the other artifacts.

"So." Aunt Laura perched herself delicately on the edge of Elaine's bed. "Do you want to hear the story?"

She opened one eye and observed her aunt with a wry smile. "You mean you're gonna tell me now?"

She opened both eyes as she pulled up a ceramic trivet, painted with little red chili peppers on a glossy white background; a souvenir from a vacation that she and Richard had taken to Santa Fe. Not a scratch on it.

"Justin never was the same after you left, honey."

Elaine nodded absently, still marveling at the trivet and how it had made its way, unscathed, into the box. Then Laura's words dawned on her.

"So his bad attitude is all my fault?" Elaine frowned. No. She wouldn't take the blame for whatever was wrong with him. Maybe tonight—seeing her again—maybe it was just a bad night for him. It hadn't exactly been a piece of cake for her either. But if five years was enough time for her to get over everything that happened, it was more than enough time for him to get over her leaving town. It wasn't as if she left him personally.

"No, of course not. But they say prison changes a man."

"Hmm." The noise she made came out sounding skeptical. That may be true, but...*Wait just a minute!* "Prison?"

Aunt Laura nodded and took a breath to continue the story.

"Justin?" The idea hit her like a slap. "Justin went to prison?"

"Yes, dear."

"But...but...he's a deputy sheriff! What for?"

"Drugs."

"What?" That absolutely could not be true. Not Justin.

"I know what you're thinking." Aunt Laura took a deep breath and let it out in a heavy sigh, as if she'd just heard the news. "But all those things they found in his house...Some kind of lab..."

Elaine blinked several times trying to dispel the image of Justin hunched over a table full of drug paraphernalia, manufacturing some illegal substance. What would he do with it when he got it made? He couldn't possibly have used it himself. "Justin's probably never even tried a cigarette. He doesn't drink.

He's a boy scout. His career—his life—is law enforcement."

"Not anymore."

Elaine felt her shoulders sag. *That explains it!* The awkwardness between Justin and Ed, the fact that he didn't work for the Sheriff's Department anymore, the complete change in him. Still...She'd known Justin her whole life. There was a time when they'd been best friends. She shook her head. It couldn't be true. There had to be more to it.

"OK, so what's the rest of the story?" Elaine set the trivet back into the box and gave Aunt Laura her full attention.

Aunt Laura only shook her head. "That's it. That's the story. Someone tipped off the police about some kind of drug lab in his garage. They raided it, arrested him. He went to court. He was convicted. Spent a year in prison."

The idea of Justin, handcuffed and fingerprinted, on trial, spending a year in a prison cell was so totally discrepant that she could only sit, too stunned to speak for a moment.

"When did he get out?"

Aunt Laura looked up at the ceiling for a second as if her next words would come from there. "July. Or maybe August of this year."

So recently. Tears surged at the thought of Justin's ordeal. She took a deep breath and tried to stem their flow. "What does he do now?"

"Construction. Odd jobs." Laura reached into the box and took out a small crystal paperweight. "He works when he can and takes care of Lorraine. He lives out in that old mobile home on the back side of her pasture."

"He lost his house?"

"He couldn't very well keep it from where he was."

"No, I guess not." Elaine stared silently into her box of trinkets for a long moment before she felt Aunt Laura give her a light pat on the thigh. Like she'd just recited the grocery list instead of detailing how a good man's life had been ruined.

"I brought you some extra blankets in case you get chilly tonight." Aunt Laura pointed to the pile at the foot of the bed. "Good night, dear."

"Night," she echoed faintly.

Listening to the sound of her aunt's footsteps, Elaine let her gaze wander back to the yearbook and her own hand which touched it almost warily. She flipped open the cover of the book and turned a few pages, reading the words written by friends and classmates, and brushing her fingertips over the photos of people she once knew. A slow smile formed.

She turned another page to see Justin's small script set neatly and compactly into the corner, next to his senior picture.

To the sweetest girl I know. It's hard to believe you'll be leaving here soon. I'll miss you a lot and I'll think of you often. Good luck in college. Let me hear from you sometimes. Justin Barnet.

A short, sardonic laugh erupted before she could stop it. The sting of tears followed quickly...*the sweetest girl*...Where had that girl gone?

He'd signed his first and last name like she wouldn't remember who he was after being gone for a few months. She touched his picture with the tip of her finger as if it could bring back the happy boy in that photo.

Another surge of tears stung her eyes and she snapped the book shut, quickly forcing them back down to their source. *No!* She would not cry. Not for herself. Not for Justin. She delved back into the box, pushing some things aside and pausing briefly to look at others. How people had known that some of these items belonged to her was anyone's guess.

Some things were obvious, like her yearbook and a photo album with pictures taken at various church functions that she had either attended or helped organize. There was a scarf that had been hers, a watch that had belonged to Richard, a pair of scissors that even she couldn't positively identify as belonging to her, numerous books and a few CD's.

At the very bottom of the box lay a photograph of Richard and her on their wedding day. The cut glass frame had been broken in three or four places, but all the pieces were there with the photograph set gently underneath them. The picture was scratched and creased, stiff and warped, with her face and that of her husband smiling from the bottom of the box that now held the last remaining fragments of the life they'd shared.

Hundreds of times she'd tried to revive this image of him in her mind and couldn't do it. She swallowed hard and sat for a moment staring at his face. She could remember his favorite color was green and his hair had been dark blond, that he'd been six foot two, and liked to play golf and monopoly and tell dumb Aggie jokes. But she hadn't been able to bring him back to life in her mind's eye, at least not for long enough to give her any comfort at all.

Yet there he was, unmistakable and almost tangible before her. There was his smile and she knew it instantly, as if she'd never lost it. As if she'd seen him only yesterday. The room around her began to spin.

She gathered up the artifacts of her previous life and shoved them roughly back into the box, burying that picture. She even put the box back up on the closet shelf where she found it.

Then she turned off the lamp on the night stand, crawled into bed, fluffed the pillows, and lay there staring at the ceiling. She listened to the sounds of the house, the chilly wind stirring the barren branches of the trees outside, and knew that box was up there on the shelf in her closet. Knew the picture of Richard waited for her to bring it out again, to look at him, alive and happy, not cold and dead as she'd remembered him these past years.

❧❦

It was either the wind whistling through the old windows or the rhythmic banging coming from downstairs that awakened Elaine. She opened eyes and listened for the noise again until she heard it, accompanied by a yelp. *Aunt Laura!*

Elaine threw back the covers and was down the hall without even putting on her slippers.

Downstairs in the kitchen, Laura struggled with the screen door as the wind whipped it open and then slammed it shut.

"Come give me a hand," Aunt Laura said, examining a fresh welt on her hand that was already beginning to bruise. "I'm trying to get it latched. I was hoping to keep from waking you."

Elaine reached for the door's small metal handle, pulled it shut, and latched it with such ease that it surprised her after having watched her aunt struggling with it. Then she reached for Laura's hand to examine the rapidly developing purple bruise.

"Let's put some ice on that." She led Aunt Laura toward the refrigerator, and after wrapping several ice cubes in a towel and pressing it gently to her hand, she gave her aunt a stern look. "Why didn't you call me? I could have done that for you."

"There was no need. I've done that a hundred times."

"You're gonna have a bad bruise."

"Honey, I'm old, I bruise easy. It's really not as bad as it looks."

Maybe the bruise wasn't going to be as bad as it looked, but in the morning light the house was clearly worse than it looked yesterday. From the stained and dingy tile on the counter tops, to the creaky, battered old floor, this kitchen showed every year of its age. The only updates had been the purchase of new appliances somewhere along the way. But even most of those had been around as long as she could remember.

Elaine yawned, stretched and looked out the back window. The dangerous and unnatural rake of the back porch seemed worse than ever. Sooner or later the whole thing would probably break right off the house and roll down the steep slope of the overgrown backyard. Then there was the old garage with its sagging door, and the apartment above it. No telling what kind of shape that place was in.

"Aunt Laura, how old is this house?" Elaine turned and leaned back against the counter.

Her aunt emptied the towel of ice into the sink and then stooped down to rummage around in a lower cabinet.

"Oh, let's see. I guess we moved into this house when I was five years old. That'd make it about seventy. Daddy had this house built. It was quite a place way back then." Aunt Laura looked around her kitchen, finally settling her gaze on the pan full of bacon she'd just set to frying. "I'm glad you brought it up because it's something I meant to discuss with you while you were home."

"What's that?" Elaine brought plates and juice glasses down out of an upper cabinet.

"This house. It's old."

Elaine nodded. "I'm with you so far."

"I'm old," Laura added, looking at her as if for some response.

Elaine grinned. "Well, I'm not gonna agree with that."

Laura smiled. "What I mean to say is, this house is big and I'm too old to keep it up any more. Besides which, I don't really want to." She paused and glanced at Elaine from the corner of her eye as she continued to turn the sizzling bacon. "I was wondering how you'd feel if I moved into that new apartment building they're putting up over behind the grocery store. It's just for *seniors* like me."

Elaine nodded. "If you'd be more comfortable there, Aunt Laura, I think that'd be a good idea. But what about the house? You couldn't just let it sit empty, could you?"

"No," Laura agreed with a shake of her head. "That's why I thought I'd sell it."

Elaine just blinked at her for a minute. "Sell it?"

"Honey, I know it's supposed to come to you." Laura scooped up the bacon with a fork and distributed it evenly between their two plates. "But I

33

live on a tight budget. I've never made a payment on this house, and if I was to move to an apartment I'd have to start paying rent. I'd need the money."

Aunt Laura cracked open one egg and then another, and they sizzled and popped in the hot bacon grease.

Elaine caught her uneasy sideways glance. "I never thought about you selling this house," she said softly.

"I know." Laura's voice was gentle. "But what will you do with it after I die, anyway? Blithe Settlement isn't your home anymore. You won't be moving into this house after I'm gone."

"No...But I never really thought about *that* happening either—you dying and all." Though why she'd never considered it she couldn't say. Most everyone else important to her had died.

Aunt Laura gave a little laugh as she lifted the fried eggs out of the pan and put them onto the plates, distracting Elaine from her bitter train of thought. She took a pitcher of orange juice and some margarine out of the refrigerator and carried them to the breakfast table.

This house had never been her home. She'd grown up in a smaller house a few blocks away. But it was always this house to which the family would come on Sundays after church. This was the kitchen where the family had prepared so many Christmas and Thanksgiving dinners back when she'd been a girl.

She'd known for quite a few years now this house would eventually come to her. Her great grandfather, an only child, had only had two daughters, Aunt Laura, and Elaine's grandmother, Elizabeth. Laura had never married nor had any children. Elizabeth only had one daughter, Elaine's mother who had, in turn, had only one daughter.

Suddenly Elaine could see so much more all around her than dingy grout, old plumbing, and rotting siding; so much more than just an old house. Her grandparents were gone as were her parents. Soon, though not too soon she hoped, her aunt would be gone as well. But this house would still be here. Only it might not belong to her family anymore.

"This house means a lot to me." Laura's words merged with Elaine's thoughts. "It means a lot to *us*, and I hate the thought of selling it. But look at it. It looks run-down. It *is* run-down. And it's hard for me to keep it up like it should be—"

"I know," Elaine said quickly. "I know it is. And I know it would be a lot easier on you if you didn't have it to mess with or worry about. I don't want you to have to keep it just because I'm suddenly a little sentimental about it. You're right. I'm never gonna live in it. I have a life in San Antonio now, such as it is. You should sell it."

"I should?" Laura sounded surprised. "I guess we don't have to make it a snap decision."

Elaine nodded. "But it's just as easy to settle it now. Plus I'm being a little bit selfish, I guess." She took a slow sip from her coffee mug. "I love you, Aunt Laura. I know it may not seem like it, as long as it took me to come home for a visit. I'm sorry for that." She paused and sighed. "But if you sell the house, it'll simplify things later. It won't be pulling me back here."

Aunt Laura tilted her head and gave her a long thoughtful look. Then she sighed. "Oh honey. Don't you know there's a lot more pulling you back here than this old house?"

3

Pink snapdragons.

What was it about pink snapdragons that went so well with this old house? Maybe it was the way the pink of the flowers and the yellow of the siding blended together with a sweet, old-fashioned hominess. Whatever it was, pink snapdragons were her annual favorite, and a gentle spring day like today was perfect for planting them.

Elaine stood and stretched her back as the late afternoon breeze picked up, toying with tendrils of her long, dark hair. She pushed the wayward strands behind her ears and glanced west.

A boiling purple and green storm, ominously beautiful, full of lighting and violence, encroached rapidly, obscuring the clear blue sky. Before she even had time to blink, to make sure her eyes hadn't deceived her, the storm had overtaken her. A funnel formed, twisting and snaking its way to the ground below, growing larger by the second. Then another, and another wound their way down, spindlier than the first, but just as destructive. All of them coming straight toward her.

Everyone was here today! Everyone was inside the house! She had to tell them what was coming. But she couldn't move. She stood riveted, rooted to the spot, unable to tear her attention away. Unable to scream.

Finally she found her feet and ran for the front porch. The wind nearly whipped the screen door off its hinges when she pulled it open. "Richard! Mom! Dad!" She ran frantically through the living room to the den where Richard, Justin and her father sat watching football.

"Honey, come sit down and watch the game with us." Richard grabbed her hand as she passed, and pulled her toward him.

"No, Richard!" Panic had so altered her voice that she didn't recognize it. "There's a tornado coming! We have to get to the shelter!"

"Come sit with us awhile," Richard drawled. "There's nothing to worry about."

"Elaine, honey." She turned toward her mother's voice. "It's almost time for supper. Could you set the table?"

"Mom, no! There's a tornado coming! We have to get out of here!"

"Don't worry, hon. We'll be OK."

"You don't understand! I saw it! It's coming for us! Please!" she begged breathlessly. "Please come with me to the shelter." She ran to the window to check the storm's progress. Trees were bending and snapping like twigs. The world outside had been thrown into chaos, but there was no detectable evidence of the storm's fury inside.

"Please!" Elaine turned back to entreat her family once again. But this wasn't her house anymore. She blinked and furrowed her brow. This wasn't right. This was Aunt Laura's house. But just a second ago..."Richard?"

"He's not here, Elaine." Justin came through the front door. His boot clad footsteps sounded heavy on the wood floor of Laura's living room. "Elaine, I've got some bad news—"

She choked back a sob, and when she spoke her voice was little more than a whisper. "Justin, where's Richard?"

"Elaine, he's gone."

She almost didn't hear the words over the sudden

groaning of the house. Glass shattered somewhere.

"Richard!" She called out to him, and turned to look for him, but Justin reached out for her.

"He's gone. But you'll be OK. I'll take care of you."

"Richard!" she cried once more before the sound of splitting beams and rafters filled her ears. The whole house seemed to twist and break right over their heads. "We have to go!" She screamed as the roof ripped violently away.

Elaine shot bolt upright, sweating and breathless. Squinting, she tried to make the room come into focus. *Where am I?* She stopped and listened, holding her breath. *There's no storm.* She was really here, on the couch where she'd laid down to read earlier.

Throwing back the afghan, she swung her legs over the edge, and buried her head in her hands. A headache throbbed at her temples. How long had it been since she'd had a tornado dream? A month? Two? She couldn't remember, but it had been awhile.

Her pulse was returning to normal, as was her breathing. It must be getting close to five o'clock judging by the dusky quality of the light filtering in through the sheer drapes.

"Elaine, help me!" A feeble cry came from the direction of the kitchen.

"Aunt Laura?"

In a replay of the event that had happened that morning, Elaine bolted toward the kitchen. The back door stood wide open, and Laura lay amidst a pile of what used to be the porch.

Laura's face was pasty pale and she had broken out into a sweat even though the temperature outside wasn't even forty degrees and she didn't have a sweater on.

"Aunt Laura, what happened?" Elaine clambered

down into the rubble. "Can you move?"

Laura shook her head and tried to prop herself up on her elbows. "I can't get up."

"Hold on! Just a minute!" Elaine rushed back inside and dialed 911. She also grabbed the throw from the couch. It would help keep Aunt Laura warm until help arrived.

∼∾

If she just hadn't fallen asleep on the couch...Elaine stretched and rubbed the back of her neck, then checked the hall once more for any sign of a doctor. If she'd stayed in the kitchen to help Aunt Laura instead of taking her suggestion to go sit down and relax, this wouldn't have happened. Just this morning she'd looked at that old rotting porch and wondered how long it would be until the thing just fell off. She should have said something about it.

With a heavy sigh, she dropped into a waiting room chair. A table beside her held an array of magazines and she sifted through them for the tenth time. Something must be really wrong. Maybe Aunt Laura had broken her leg, or her hip. It wouldn't be taking so long for someone to come fill her in on the situation otherwise.

"Oh! Here you are!"

Elaine glanced up from the magazines in time to see Mrs. Barnet hobbling as swiftly as she could towards her. Right on her heels followed a dour-looking Justin. The sight of him brought her recent dream vividly to mind, but before she could shake the image, Mrs. Barnet sat down, set her cane aside, and clasped both hands.

"What happened?" Mrs. Barnet's eyes filled with something near terror.

Elaine shrugged and shook her head. "She went outside to get the broom, and that old back porch just collapsed. She hurt one of her legs. The paramedics worried that she might have broken something, but I haven't spoken with a doctor yet."

Justin sat down across from them and leaned forward, balancing elbows on knees, both hands in front of him. His gaze stayed on his old boots.

Elaine dragged her own gaze from him back to his mother.

"Ed Lacey heard the dispatcher on his radio and called Dot. Dot called me and asked if I could come check on you. She'll be along a little later on."

"Thank you for coming, Mrs. Barnet." Elaine squeezed her hands gratefully. "And thank you for coming, too, Justin."

Justin looked up when she said his name. "No problem."

"Well, we'll just sit and wait with you." Mrs. Barnet picked up a magazine and flipped through its pages.

Elaine cast a covert glance at Justin to find him staring at the floor again. Could he have spent any time thinking about all the good times they'd had together not so many years ago, regretting all that had happened to make them such total strangers to each other now?

She glanced at the clock. What could be taking so long? She pushed up out of the seat to check the hall and found a doctor emerging from the emergency room corridor and coming her way.

"Hi, Lorriane. Justin." The doctor greeted them

both with a handshake as he stepped into the waiting room. Then extended his hand to her. "And you must be Elaine."

She shook his hand. "Yes. Hi."

"I'm Boyd Wendall." He smiled gently. "It's good to finally meet you. I've been your aunt's doctor for about four years now."

Elaine offered a smile, though it felt strained. "How is she?"

Dr. Wendall smiled. "She's doing just fine. She has a pretty badly sprained ankle. And a couple of lacerations that needed stitching that we'll have to keep an eye on. But nothing's broken. No concussion."

Elaine hadn't even known she held her breath until she let it out in a long relieved sigh. "So she'll be OK?"

Dr. Wendall seemed to think for a second. "Well, the sprain and the wounds won't heal as fast as they would in a younger patient. And some physical therapy may be in order. I'd like to keep her overnight just to monitor her a little more. But she should make a full recovery." He paused and grinned. "Which is more than I can say for the porch, judging from the way she described it."

Elaine smiled gratefully. "Can I see her?"

He nodded. "She's in some pain, but we're giving her something for that. I'm having her admitted and moved into a room. The receptionist can tell you where she is."

"Thank you, Dr. Wendall." She reached out to shake his hand, and he clasped it warmly in both of his.

"Call me Boyd."

She nodded. "Thank you."

He laid his hand on her shoulder, tilting his head, obviously trying to maintain eye contact. "Let me know if there's anything I can do for you, OK?"

"OK. Thanks." Her response came out uncharacteristically soft. She almost cringed, glancing away. In doing so she caught a glimpse of Justin and the look on his face. What was it...irritation, annoyance? No, it was disgust.

He covered it quickly and looked down.

❧⚘

Dr. Wendall was already in Laura's room when Elaine, Lorraine and Justin got there.

"Well." He handed a clipboard to a waiting nurse. "I'll just let y'all get settled. Be sure and let us know if there's anything else you need." He met Elaine's gaze briefly and smiled, then turned back to Aunt Laura. "I'll be back in to check on you tomorrow morning."

"Thank you, Doctor." Aunt Laura watched him go, then relaxed back against her pillows.

"That's some doctor you got there." Elaine pulled a chair up next to Laura's bed.

"Isn't he?" Laura's voice sounded bright, although she still looked pale, and she grimaced as she tried to shift in the bed. "He's single, you know. Wouldn't he make a good catch?"

Elaine tried to hide a grin and arranged Aunt Laura's pillow behind her. "I think he's a little young for you, Aunt Laura."

Her aunt made a cheeky noise and dismissed the comment with a wave of her hand as a nurse placed a tray on a roll away cart and positioned it in front of Aunt Laura. "I hear someone hasn't had her supper yet."

"You know I think I could eat a bite." Aunt Laura tried to shift again as the nurse uncovered her entrée; a bland looking little piece of chicken and rice. "Elaine, did you get some supper?"

Elaine shook her head, but her stomach growled. She *must* be hungry if the sight of hospital food made her want to eat. "I'm all right. I'll get something later."

"No ma'am. You go get something now. You haven't eaten since lunch and that was hours ago. I won't have you wasting away while you're home."

"Really, I'd rather stay here with you."

"Don't be silly. Lorraine is here with me."

"Yes!" Mrs. Barnet chimed in. "I'll stay until you get back. Justin will go with you."

Elaine raised one hand to her temple and tried to rub the persistent ache away. "I'm fine—"

Mrs. Barnet set her cane aside, came across the room, grabbed Justin by one arm and Elaine by the other, and ushered them both to the door. "Go on now. There's a cafeteria on the first floor."

Elaine grabbed for her purse, barely managing to snag her coat along with it. *Crippling arthritis, huh?* She turned with a wry comment for Justin on the tip of her tongue, only to find that he'd already made it halfway to the elevators. She hurried to catch up.

The elevator door slid closed and silence engulfed them. She took a deep breath and held it, letting her eyes drift closed momentarily, hoping to relieve the stress of this afternoon. But an image assaulted her, of Richard smiling, green eyes sparkling with humor, morning light reflecting off his fair stubble as he raised a cup of coffee for a sip. Another image quickly followed, of that same dear face, eyes closed in death, the last time she'd seen it before the funeral director had ordered his casket closed forever.

"You OK?" Justin's voice broke the silence.

Elaine let the breath out in a quick rush and nodded, but a tear slid down her cheek anyway.

"It sounds like your aunt's going to be fine."

Elaine opened her eyes and swiped at the errant tear. "I know. It's just…" She let her voice trail off with a shake of her head. Now the urgency of Aunt Laura's accident had worn off, now it was clear she'd be OK and her injuries weren't as severe as the paramedics had feared, now this hospital's other memories assailed her. "I just hate hospitals." She offered him a feeble smile. "Do you mind if we don't go to the cafeteria?"

His expression softened into a look of complete understanding, which did nothing to help keep her composure. "How does a burger sound?"

She swallowed and looked down, nodding because she couldn't speak.

The elevator doors slid open and they stepped off. Justin slowed his pace and stayed beside her as they walked to his truck in silence. He opened the passenger side door. She reached for the armrest on the door and put one foot on the chrome step bar, ready to climb into the cab. But then she stalled.

In that instant all the details her aunt told her last night began to swirl like smoke, clouding her previously unshakable faith and trust in him. He'd been in prison. Arrested and convicted on drug charges. Last night she'd been sure it had been a mistake. He *had* to be innocent. But what if he wasn't? What kind of man had he turned into these past few years? She glanced up at his face.

Perfect Shelter

"Is something wrong?" The utterly injured expression in his eyes contradicted his defensive tone. As if he'd read her mind.

She shook her head and looked down quickly. "No."

She climbed into the red quad cab he'd purchased new a year before she'd left. He'd been so proud of it. It had been his first new truck, and he'd driven it out to their house the day he bought it to show it to her and Richard. Really just Richard, probably. It was a nice truck. But she didn't have the same appreciation for it another guy would. A faint smile touched her lips, and her heart. Justin had even let Richard drive it.

She ran one finger along a small rip in the upholstery on the edge of the bench seat. Now it was just another old truck, with scratches in the paint, chips in the windshield, and dents in the fenders. There was nothing special about it anymore.

"So has your aunt talked to you about sellin' the house, yet?" The sound of his voice startled her.

"Um...as a matter of fact, we discussed it just this morning." She ran a hand through her hair, realizing suddenly that she'd come straight here from her nap on the living room couch. "Why do you ask?"

"Oh, you know, she and Mom are pretty good friends. Your Aunt Laura was running the idea by her not long before you got here. I was kind of wondering what she was up to."

She nodded, watching the buildings on the main drag go by with their Christmas lights ablaze.

"I was thinking that maybe you could take this whole incident today as a sign from God. Like maybe this is the time to sell it."

Elaine couldn't suppress a short, blunt, and very

45

bitter laugh—not that she tried. "Well, if *this* is a sign from God, then I guess it's about par for the course."

Justin looked sharply at her, then returned his attention to the road. But he didn't say anything else until they pulled into the parking lot of the Prickly Pear Cafe.

"I think it's hard on your Aunt, being in that big old house by herself."

"I know it is." She felt around for the door handle, hoping to just jump out of the truck, ending this conversation before it could begin. She'd seen today the dangers inherent in Aunt Laura's continuing to live alone. She really didn't need the lecture. The throbbing behind her eyes suddenly doubled its intensity.

"Just think what might have happened if you hadn't been there when that porch gave out under her. And it was gonna happen. She probably goes out on that porch for something every day."

How would you know what she does every day? She had to bite her tongue as all her angry defenses went up, aided by the guilt that she had been asleep when the porch collapsed. *She* should have been the one going out for the broom. Not her seventy-five year old great aunt. "I haven't been thinking about much else this evening."

Judging by the glower he gave her, he'd heard the note of displeasure in her voice. But he wasn't finished.

"You know, you don't live here anymore and you probably won't be here if something like this ever happens again." He paused and took a breath, jerking his keys from the ignition. His tone had grown more condemning with each word. "That old house is a burden for her, and I don't think you should expect her to hang onto it just because you stand to inherit it one day."

"Look, Justin," she snapped as the pounding in her head grew particularly fierce. "I *know* I don't live here anymore. I left on purpose and it was one of the best decisions I ever made. I don't intend to come back here, and I know that Aunt Laura doesn't want to live alone anymore. She and I have already talked about this. And you know what? I don't really *care* what you think. And this is none of your business, anyway."

She ended by releasing a long, angry breath. She shoved a hand through her hair, and then pressed both palms to her eyes to block out the stabbing neon glare from the Prickly Pear's open sign. Another breath, this one more calming, eased her nerves a little. Then a wave of remorse swept over her. She didn't want to fight with him. She'd been so happy to see him last night. She wanted to talk to him as a friend, but his resentment had made her defensive.

"I'm sorry, Justin." She reached over and laid a conciliatory hand on his arm and sensed his tension diminish some. "I didn't mean that. I *do* care what you think, and I know you're thinking about what's best for Aunt Laura. She and I have talked all through this. And it might surprise you to know that I encouraged her to sell the house. Just this morning, in fact. I mean, you're right. It's not fair to expect her to continue to live in that big old house just because I'll inherit it one day. I'd just sell it, anyway."

"Oh." If that was disappointment she detected in his response, he covered it quickly as he turned for the handle of his door.

"But tonight I've been thinking." She stopped him with her voice. "I sat there in the hospital, picturing Aunt Laura in some old nursing home, using a wheel chair or a walker, and I thought maybe I *could* move back here, into the house with her. Just until she can get around on her own. She's gonna need someone there with her for now, anyway. Right? And if she wants to sell it, it could use a little sprucing up. She'll need help arranging that."

"Don't you have a life in San Antonio? A job?"

She shrugged and shook her head. "I can get a job anywhere. My rental contract is up at the end of this month anyway, and I've been wanting to find another place." She laughed humorlessly. "Everything I own fits quite nicely in the trunk of my car and a small U-Haul trailer."

It would take a one day trip to relocate. She wouldn't even have to spend the night. Rootless is what she'd wanted to be when she left here. And that's what she was. And when Aunt Laura was up and around, and settled into her new apartment with her house neatly sold, she'd be free to go wherever she wanted.

"Elaine, what have you been doing the past five years?"

He sat on the other side of the truck cab examining every little groove in one of his keys instead of looking at her, but sounding like he sincerely needed to know. She took a deep breath and tried hard to control her voice when she spoke.

"I haven't been doing much of anything. I've waited tables, sold shoes, cleaned houses, secretarial work...Just tried to get by mostly."

He nodded.

The sun had set hours ago and dark, chilly night surrounded them. Elaine rubbed her hands together to fight off the chill. Light from the red neon "Open" sign in the front window of the diner mixed with flickering fluorescent tubes under the front awning to provide enough light for her to see Justin's blue gaze when he raised it to meet hers.

"But did you accomplish what you meant to when you left here? Did it help at all?"

She swallowed. *Had* she accomplished what she'd set out to when she ran away? Had she intended to accomplish anything aside from leaving? She'd never thought too hard about why she picked up her purse and got onto a bus headed out of town that day. Maybe it had been shock. Maybe it had been her anger with God that caused her to abandon the place to which He'd called her, and Him. If she'd meant to leave all the feelings behind; the anger, the grief, the bitterness—she'd failed. As hard as she'd tried to feel nothing the past five years, those things had followed her.

She sighed and let the weariness seep into her every fiber. "You thinking of running away, Justin? Now that your mom is getting remarried and won't need you quite so much? Are you thinkin' that maybe now's your chance to get away from here and start over someplace else?"

He gave his head a quick shake and reached for the door handle. "An arrest record has a way of following you, so it wouldn't matter if I did, anyway."

4

"Ow!" Elaine dropped the screwdriver and shook her hand. She examined now bleeding knuckles. This made the fourth or fifth time she'd scraped them on the frame of the bed which, fortunately for her poor hands, was now reassembled.

Aunt Laura would be coming home tomorrow, but wouldn't be able to manage the stairs for another few weeks. So Elaine had spent the better part of this morning clearing books and bookshelves out of this old room and wrestling her aunt's disassembled full size bed down the stairs a piece at a time. She looked around the small back room, which up until now had been used for storage. It had a closet and was right across the hall from the laundry room and next door to a three-quarter bathroom. It still needed a good cleaning, especially the carpet.

Elaine glanced at her watch. Aunt Laura was expecting her in an hour. That left enough time to stop by the hardware store to rent a carpet cleaning machine. She'd visit her aunt, then come home and spend the night cleaning up this room. It'd be better than sleeping, dreaming of tornados.

She pushed off the floor, gathered tools, and headed for the laundry room where her aunt's bedding was drying. She had enough time to get the bed made before she left.

The sound of a car door slamming out back made her jump. She passed through the laundry room, into the kitchen and peeked out the window.

Justin had parked his truck and stood surveying the back porch—or what was left of it. He walked around it, hands stuffed into the pockets of his old, worn jacket, kicking debris with a boot clad foot.

His defenses were down, the lines of his face relaxed. His expression was almost pleasant. His eyes almost sparkled.

A sudden yearning tore through bringing the sting of tears. There was so much she wanted to say to him. She wanted to tell him everything she'd done these past years and she wanted desperately to hear his story.

Their last conversation had been strained and awkward. No, make that adversarial. Shame stung anew when she thought of how defensive she'd been when he'd only been thinking of what was best for her aunt. They ended up ordering their burgers and eating in relative silence, with nothing more of significance said between them. She'd had so many questions, but Justin had sunk deeply into his own thoughts, and she hadn't the right to intrude. But she wanted to sit and talk with him, like they used to. Back when they were kids. She still craved his friendship.

The feeling propelled her through the kitchen to the back door where she paused, hand poised on the knob. Maybe she should just leave him alone. There was no way they would just pick up where they left off, friendship intact. Too much had happened to him in her absence, and he resented her for leaving. Maybe she should just leave well enough alone. But she couldn't.

Elaine pulled the door open, and felt an odd catch in her chest when he met her gaze.

"Hi." She tried to smile.

He looked back down at the porch. "Hi. Sorry, didn't know you'd be here. I told your Aunt Laura that I'd come out and have a look at the porch. See if I can put it back together."

"Can I get you anything?" Elaine had to clear a catch out of her throat. "Coffee?"

Justin shook his head.

Elaine stepped down, testing each spot gingerly, before she put her full weight down. A board creaked and gave way so she quickly changed her course. He reached out a hand to steady her and she grabbed it reflexively, holding on as she made her way through the rubble.

"So, what do you think? Can it be fixed?"

Justin shook his head, letting her hand go as soon as she reached solid ground. "Wouldn't be any point trying to fix it. It's rotten all through." He picked up a splintered fragment, crumbled it like a cracker in his hands, and watched the remains fall silently to the ground. He dusted his hands off on his jeans. "You'd be better off replacing it with a whole new porch."

"What's that likely to cost?"

Justin shrugged. "I'll do it for you for the cost of materials, if you don't mind that I may need to leave it for awhile to go out on another job."

"No!" Elaine held up a hand to interrupt him. "We couldn't let you do it for nothing."

He held up his hand mirroring her gesture. "Miss Laura was a good friend to my mother and a big help while I was...away." He shook his head. "I insist."

Elaine swallowed the lump in her throat and

nodded.

"I can bring you an estimate tomorrow morning. I could probably get started on it after New Year's Day."

Elaine smiled. "Thank you, Justin."

He looked down when she said his name, then examined the porch and siding.

"So what's your professional opinion of the house as a whole?" She stepped over to see what he was looking at.

"It could use some work."

Elaine laughed.

When he looked at her, he had an unconscious smile on his face. The sight of it nearly took her breath away. "It's falling apart, Justin. Literally." She indicated the porch with a nod. "It's OK, you can say it."

He smiled again, deliberately this time, but just as honestly.

"Well." He toed the rubble at his feet, then glanced back at her. "It's maybe not what you remember from when you were a girl. It's old and a little run down. But it's not that bad."

"But it needs work."

"Yeah. But what old house doesn't? It can be done."

Elaine nodded. "Fixing the biggest problems—like the porch here—would probably make the place a little easier to sell, when the time comes. Don't you think?"

Justin took a deep breath and seemed to consider for a moment. He nodded slowly. "Every little bit helps. I take it you had no trouble convincing your aunt that you should come back for awhile."

Elaine shrugged then shook her head. "If I didn't know better, I'd suspect she had the whole thing planned all along, right down to the part where she destroyed the porch and nearly destroyed her ankle."

In fact, if she didn't know better she'd suspect this was just the first step in a grander, more diabolical plan on her aunt's part to get her back here for good.

∂∾∾

"Oh, Elaine, please! You just can't say 'no' to a poor old crippled woman."

Elaine looked skeptically at her aunt who sat, propped up against a stack of fluffy pillows, wrapped snugly in her red and green plaid fleece bathrobe. She pulled an heirloom Christmas quilt over her aunt's legs to her waist. "Why can't I?"

"Elaine, you *have* to go!"

Elaine could have easily fired back yet another impertinent remark, and she would have, too, if Laura hadn't looked so precariously close to tears.

The subject was church. Elaine hadn't dealt with it in five years and was finding patience hard to maintain. The Christmas Eve candle light service was tonight and Aunt Laura, as usual, had been involved in the organization of the event since before Thanksgiving.

"Elaine, I'm supposed to go help get the sanctuary ready and hand out candles and programs. Obviously, *I* can't go. But I don't want the others to be short handed."

"They'll manage." Elaine turned from the bed and began gathering up the various toiletries and cosmetics she'd brought to her aunt's bedside when Laura had insisted that, even if she was confined to a bed, she wouldn't look all bedraggled on Christmas Eve.

"They *won't* manage!" Her aunt folded arms across her chest, and her sullen, pouty expression almost made Elaine laugh. "They're old women. Their minds are going and they need someone to be in charge."

"And that someone is you?" Elaine raised her eyebrows.

"Well, in my absence, I guess that someone will have to be *you*."

"And how would that look, my leaving you all alone with your injuries on Christmas Eve?"

"Oh, stop thinking of yourself," Laura said smartly, half kidding, half serious judging by the look on her face.

Elaine couldn't stifle her laugh. But it soon faded into silence. The last time she'd been to the church had been after Richard's funeral. She'd gone to collect all his personal things from the office. She swallowed down the ache forming at the memory of how she'd packed up all his books, papers, and photographs, sobbing shamelessly.

Elaine took a breath and steeled herself. "I just can't." Her voice sounded sharper than she'd intended. She tried to correct it with a smile and a gentler tone. "I can't go back into that building. I don't *want* to."

"But, honey, it's Christmas. What better time to—"

"No." Elaine shook her head.

"If you won't do it for you, then do it for me." Laura said. "Do it as a favor to your old, broken aunt who can't fulfill her obligations for tonight. You won't ever have to go again if you don't want to."

"Aunt Laura..." She let her voice trail off after realizing the words had come out sounding harsher than she'd intended. She sighed. "Please don't ask it of me. I just can't."

↪↩

Elaine drew in a deep shaky breath of chilly late afternoon air and let it out again in a puff of vapor. She pulled her coat tighter and shivered. She and Aunt Laura had gone around about it this afternoon. In the end guilt had driven her to agree to go to church in her aunt's place.

She stared up at the big, wooden double doors that would allow passage into the foyer and, beyond that, the sanctuary. Where her husband had delivered his sermons. She reached out for the iron rail beside her as a torrent of memories streamed over her. Her knees felt dangerously close to buckling, just as they'd done when she had first observed her husband's corpse. She locked them and stiffened her spine.

Even with all the memories, the only lingering image she could recall of Richard was his lifeless body on a stretcher, a crisp white sheet pulled back only far enough to see his face. Enough for her to know without a doubt that news of his death had not been a mistake and God really had taken him from her.

Elaine took another deep breath, pulled open the door, and stepped inside, trembling.

The quiet bustle of the women in the sanctuary surrounded her as they dusted and tidied up the pews, and put the finishing touches on the Christmas decorations. The activity stopped before Elaine realized it. One by one, the women had paused what they were doing and stood watching her. Elaine took another deep breath and reached for the back of a pew, something tangible and solid to lean on.

"Elaine Mallory!" Mrs. Simon sounded positively joyful.

Five years ago Mrs. Simon had sold her a bus ticket to Dallas with a sad, confused expression. Now she looked ecstatic to see Elaine. She pulled her into a tight hug.

"I was so sorry I missed Laura's party. Especially after I heard you'd come back to town. It's so good to see you, dear. We've missed you."

Elaine smiled as warmly as she could. "Thank you."

"And how is Laura? Is she home from the hospital?"

She nodded. "Yes. She's well. Just not up to being here tonight. So she sent me to fill in."

Mrs. Simon's brows knit together as she studied Elaine, but then she put her to work folding programs and hunting down the small candles which managed to get misplaced every year. Having some task to do calmed her nerves, but then the women dimmed the sanctuary lights for the service. As the first worshippers came trickling in, her hands began to tremble again.

Before Elaine could get away, Mrs. Simon assigned her the honor of handing out candles as congregation members came steadily in to take their places.

Boyd Wendall came in alone, and his face lit up with a warm smile when he saw her. "Elaine. It's good to see you again. How is Laura? Is she settled in well at home?"

Elaine nodded. "Feisty as ever." She handed candles to a couple she didn't recognize. Dr. Wendall stepped aside, but didn't leave to take his seat.

"And you?"

She glanced down into the box of candles, avoiding the interest and sympathy she saw in his expression. Clearly he knew her story. She forced a smile. "I'll be fine."

"Are you alone?" He swallowed. "You could sit with me during the service."

"Thank you, Dr. Wendall, but I wasn't planning on staying for the service. I'm just filling in for Aunt Laura." She bit her lower lip to stop the tears and kept her gaze fixed on the jumble of candles in her box. Then she felt his hand on her elbow.

"Call me Boyd," he said softly. "Please."

She nodded.

He smiled encouragingly and turned to take his seat.

Elaine drew in a deep breath trying to tamp emotions down. And when she looked up again, there was Justin, looking grim. She swallowed and tried to clear the lump from her throat as he ushered his mother through the foyer to receive their candles. The lines of his face were hard and he leveled a penetrating, oddly accusatory stare at her. Elaine offered a feeble quivery smile, and he softened. Before she could look away from him, Mrs. Barnet swept her into a warm hug.

"Elaine, honey, it's so good to see you. What are you doing here?"

She dragged her gaze from Justin's face to Mrs. Barnet's. "Aunt Laura sent me to..." She let her voice trail off before it could crack and humiliate her.

Justin's mother patted Elaine's shoulder. "Oh, you're such a good girl for helping out. I know it can't be easy for you."

Elaine swallowed that lump again and looked

down at the candles. Finally, a little compassion. Tears stung her eyes, but she blinked them away.

Mrs. Barnet stepped past her, and Justin moved up. Elaine raised her gaze to find him studying her face in such an apologetic way that she had to look down again to control already raw emotions. She extended her hand, but realized the mistake when his hand closed tightly and warmly around hers.

Elaine swallowed and tried to meet his gaze, but found she couldn't. Instead, she pulled her hand from his grasp and gave him a candle. When she finally looked at him, his expression wasn't readable.

It was the same way he'd looked that terrible day when he'd stood on her front porch bearing the news of her husband's death. It could have been pain, regret, or maybe compassion that she saw in his eyes, she couldn't tell which. Whatever the actual emotion was, the tears lurking there were unmistakable, though they didn't fall.

They both looked down.

"Thanks," Justin said, his voice rough and almost inaudible.

Elaine took a deep, steadying breath as he stepped past her, then she greeted the next person in line.

Come on, keep the line moving. Let's go, people. The sooner everyone got seated, the sooner the service could start. The sooner she could be out of here.

Coming back to Blithe Settlement had been a mistake. Deciding to stay, even temporarily had been a huge mistake. But she'd already told Aunt Laura of her plans to stay, so she didn't know how she could back out now. Her best course would probably be to get into her car and just drive away. But something inside whispered, *"Stay."*

❧❧

Dingy incandescent light spilled onto the beat up, brown carpeting of Justin's old mobile home when he clicked on the lamp next to the front door. He shrugged off his jacket, tossed it onto the back of a chair and turned to check his answering machine for messages. Not that he expected to find any. Not on Christmas Eve. No one would be calling him with work tonight.

Work had slowed the past two months since the weather started turning colder, but it didn't make much difference to him financially. The mobile home belonged to his mother and was on her property, so the utilities would be paid this month. Living so close to her also meant that he wouldn't go hungry. But soon she'd be married again, and he needed to find another place. The last thing he wanted was to be underfoot and in the way.

Being between jobs was wearing on his nerves and his checking account. But mostly it was wearing on his pride. There were no messages from either of the two local contractors he liked to work for. No messages resulting from the business card he'd put up on the bulletin board outside the grocery store or from the occasional add he ran in the *Thrifty Nickel*. There was no *paying* work.

He sank down into his recliner and fished a little piece of paper out of his shirt pocket. It was a check Laura had given him to buy lumber for her new back porch. He'd have no trouble finishing it quickly as long as no one called him to go on a paying job. He turned the check over with his fingers a few times and then set it on the end table.

There were few remnants of his old life here; a few bits of furniture that he'd been able to hang onto, some photographs, dishes, his television and CD player. He hadn't had much to begin with. But he'd had a small house, a place of his own; a good start in life.

Justin shook his head. He tried not to think about all that. *This* is where he lived now. *This* was his life. Everything that happened before—Elaine, Richard, prison—that was over and unchangeable. He made a conscious effort not to dwell on it. Nothing good could happen if he gave in to the overwhelming urge to investigate and try to prove who hated him enough to hurt him.

He tried to shake the train of thought from his head. There weren't too many things more pathetic than a thirty year old man living off his widowed and disabled mother. It would have been easier if he'd been able to run away like Elaine. But since his father passed away, his mother needed him as much as he relied on her. And when he'd been working successfully in the only job he'd ever really wanted, he'd had joy in taking care of her. Now, she was taking care of him.

On the end table lay his open Bible. It had lain there untouched the past few days. He still read from it occasionally and attended church on Sundays. Mostly he found comfort in it. But he couldn't overcome the feeling that God had forgotten him.

He picked up the Bible and let his eyes find the last verses he had read.

...And we rejoice in the hope of the glory of God. Not only so, but we also rejoice in our sufferings, because we know that suffering produces perseverance; perseverance, character; and character, hope.

Justin never pretended to know why God had

allowed his life to turn in the direction it had. To fall from where he'd been to where he was now was nearly unbearable. The year spent in prison under the supervision of correctional officers who knew he'd once been on their side of the law had been torment.

Justin closed his eyes against the memory of how he'd once argued his innocence to one.

"Yeah," the CO had responded with a snide chuckle and thinly veiled sneer. *"You all say that, don't you? You're all innocent as little white doves. That's why you're here."*

He'd never mentioned it again.

He opened his eyes and surveyed his present reality. He'd given up on finding justice. With a district attorney and judge determined to make an example of him, COs who considered him worse than a common criminal, and no one with the means of fighting for him, justice was unattainable. And now, righting those wrongs would be pointless. Even if he were to find the justice he craved, it wouldn't change anything that happened.

Every so often the urge to fight would surge. When he'd had enough of the sympathy in people's eyes, or when they whispered to visiting friends and relatives as they passed him on the street. But most especially when they shook their heads, like his poor, pathetic life was a shame.

Justin heaved a weary sigh and picked up Laura's check. He kept waiting for God to turn his life around and restore the position he once had. But the longer he waited, the more he just kept right on sinking.

5

Elaine squeezed her eyes shut and pinched the bridge of her nose as if the action could magically change Aunt Laura's check ledger, despite the hour she'd just spent calculating and recalculating. She opened her eyes and looked down at the booklet on the kitchen table. The deficit remained. As did the incessant sound of Justin's nail gun outside.

Gratitude swelled every time she thought of the sacrifice he was making to fix the porch for them. But surely it was time for a coffee break or something.

She leaned back against the chair and picked up a pencil, tapping it on the tabletop as she surveyed all the stuff in this room her aunt managed to accumulate. One would never guess that Aunt Laura was poor.

Well, maybe not poor in the destitute sense of the word. But definitely broke.

Elaine couldn't remember her aunt ever having a job. But clearly she had. The retirement and social security checks proved it. She shuffled through six months worth again. The two monthly checks together didn't equal what Elaine had made in wages and tips when she'd waited tables at the Alamo Cafe—and no one would consider *that* a comfortable living.

She stretched a kink out of her back and flipped a few pages in the ledger. Somehow Aunt Laura had managed to make ends meet until a couple of months ago, when her insurance payments had gone up. She'd been transferring money out of her savings account to get by since then. Elaine picked up the savings ledger. This account wasn't much healthier. But it would have to get them through one more month until she could find a job.

Elaine massaged her temples and shot a quick glance over at her aunt as she limped through the door with her walker. The rhythm of the nail gun outside continued in perfect synchronicity with the throbbing in her head. She took a long, deep breath and let it out slowly. "Know anyone who has a job opening I might be able to fill?"

Laura shrugged and sighed, obviously aware of the problem. "I can't think of anyone right off hand."

"Guess I'll start asking around on Monday. Surely I can find a job waiting tables."

"Honey, you've got a college degree. That has to qualify you for something that pays better than a waitressing job."

If only it did. "It's been ten years since I finished college and I don't have experience doing much else." Elaine took a sip of her room temperature coffee, grimaced, and got up to pour it out. "Besides, this isn't exactly a white collar town. And it's just until spring."

"Still," Laura continued thoughtfully, "maybe you should pay a visit to Darla at the Workforce Commission. Maybe she could find you a job."

Elaine nodded and again tried to massage away the pressure at her temples. "It's worth a try. God knows I hated waiting tables."

"Yes, He does."

Elaine bit her tongue. Laura had never approved of any conversation that used God's name lightly. The admonishment was quiet and not unkind, but it chafed anyway. And the unremitting sound of the construction outside was on the verge of making her shout something completely inappropriate.

Suddenly it stopped. Elaine started at the abrupt silence. She took a deep breath, held it for a moment, then let it out slowly as she crossed to the window.

Justin held a level against one board and then another, then stood up straight, rubbed his back and stretched.

"Why don't you take him a cup of coffee?"

Elaine jumped again at the sound of Laura's voice.

"It's early still, and I bet he hasn't had a cup this morning."

She tried to ignore the odd twisty feeling at the thought of sitting with him for a minute or two. Tried even harder to ignore the little voice that told her it was just the thing she ought to do. "He doesn't want to be bothered. And if he wanted a cup of coffee he'd have asked."

"No one ever bothers him," Laura said gently. "So I bet he wouldn't mind. And he's too polite to just come right up to the back door and ask for a cup of coffee. Who would do something like that? You go offer him one. And take a fresh one for yourself, too."

Elaine stood watching him, hesitant. *Best not to reconnect with him too much*. The thought came to her as clearly as it had the night she'd seen him at Aunt Laura's party.

"Go!" Her aunt's voice sounded stern. "Don't make me get up out of this chair with my injuries."

"OK." Elaine relented and poured two mugs full, doctored them both with a little milk and sugar, and turned toward the back door.

"And ask him if he'll come inside and have lunch with us later."

Elaine shot her aunt a glance and hooked the door with her foot to swing it closed.

Justin turned his head a little from where he sat on the porch, but he didn't turn around to look at her.

She took a silent breath, confused by this nervousness. She'd grown up with Justin, had sat by him, talked to him, hundreds of times. She knew him well. In fact, she probably knew him better than she knew anyone at this point, which was really sad considering the wide gulf between them now. But suddenly the thought of sitting next to him and having an unspecified conversation tied her stomach into knots.

"Coffee?" She almost cringed at the timidity in her voice as she offered him a cup.

He looked at her, squinting against the sun, and reached to accept it. "Thanks."

"Um...Do you have plans for lunch?" Her voice still sounded soft and shy. She cleared her throat.

"Thought maybe I'd go get a burger or somethin'."

"Would you like to join us?" That sounded good, relaxed, controlled. "We'll probably be having soup and sandwiches about noon. It's the least we can do for all your help."

Justin shook his head. "That's OK. You don't need to go to any trouble."

"It's no trouble." Elaine spoke quickly. She hadn't meant the offer to sound like payment on a debt rather than a personal invitation. "We'd like you to have lunch with us. We'd enjoy your company."

"All right then." He nodded as she sat down next to him.

Elaine followed his gaze toward the backyard and cradled the mug in her hands. Its warmth against the chill in the morning air was nice. She took a sip, casting a furtive glance over the rim at Justin.

The green in his plaid flannel shirt made his eyes seem even bluer than usual. *Baby blue.* The most beautiful, soulful eyes she'd ever seen. Why hadn't she reciprocated his feelings for her back in school? She'd been such a foolish girl.

He raised his cup to his mouth and she looked away quickly. "So...um...how's it goin' out here?" She glanced back over at him, watching the movement of his throat as he swallowed his coffee.

"Good."

"You've made quick progress."

He nodded. "The weather's been nice. Not too cold. It's an easy job."

"Well, it looks a lot better."

"Maybe this one'll last another seventy or so years."

"Maybe." Elaine grinned. "But will we?"

"Maybe." He mirrored her grin but still didn't look at her.

She turned to look out toward the backyard again as he took another sip of his coffee. *What is the matter with me?* This was Justin. They had lots in common. Why couldn't she think of anything to say beyond the sort of dull chit-chat that wouldn't have interested him back in high school when he was head over heels for her?

"Hope you take it with milk and sugar." She tried to push hair behind her ears with one hand, but the short bangs fell right back over her forehead. "I didn't know, so I just fixed it like I like mine."

Justin nodded. "It's good. I usually take it however it's served." He drained his cup and set it on the porch.

Elaine picked it up and rose to go inside. Disappointment swelled irritatingly at the stupid little conversation she'd just had. "Guess I better go check on Aunt Laura. Make sure she's not trying to scrub the floor or anything."

"She sent you out here, didn't she?"

Elaine stopped, hand poised to pull the back door open so she could disappear inside. It wasn't really a question. Justin sounded as if he only wanted confirmation of what he already knew.

"She...encouraged me to come out here. It's not like I didn't *want* to, Justin. It's not like I wasn't thinking about it, anyway. "

He turned and looked at her.

"It's more like she read my mind." She met his gaze momentarily and smiled before she turned toward the door. "Lunch at noon?"

Justin nodded and pushed off the porch. "I'll be here."

⁂

Justin watched her disappear and felt a slow smile spread across his face.

Was she nervous about talking to him just now?

He didn't have a whole lot of experience with women. There had been a few he'd dated through the years. But he'd never been able to seriously commit to one because it had always been Elaine he'd loved. One or two girls had acted a little like she just had—like they couldn't think of anything to say. But Elaine?

He let the thought sit for a moment more before dismissing it with a shake of his head. *Nah.* Not Elaine. They'd been friends too long for her to act that way around him. He felt his smile fade. More likely her aunt had sent her out here for the sake of hospitality. She was probably just being nice.

And the lunch invitation...*It's the least we can do for all your help*...He shook his head and grabbed his tape measure. She was just being nice. What interest could she possibly have in him? Especially now, after all that had happened. He'd been the one who told her that her husband was dead. He'd been there, within yards of Richard when the current had pulled him under, and hadn't been able to help him. He'd spent a year in prison, lost his job, his home. What did he have to offer? Especially when there was a doctor so clearly interested in her. She wasn't planning on staying any longer than it took for her aunt to heal and for the house to sell.

She'd be gone again within six months, more than likely. Maybe sooner.

He squatted to take the next measurement. No. She was just being polite on Laura's behalf. Let her have her few weeks of fun with Wendall. Maybe he could at least distract her from her painful memories. Justin knew his presence would never do anything but remind her. She'd never loved him as anything other than a friend, anyway. *Good old dependable Justin.*

Still, it was nice to feel hope again.

6

"Sorry!" Elaine winced sympathetically as she pressed a warm, wet cloth to the wound on Aunt Laura's leg. One of the big lacerations from her accident on the porch had somehow come open and began to ooze. "Did you bump it on something?"

Aunt Laura leaned back on the couch, her legs propped up on a footstool that Elaine had pulled to her.

"I don't know." Aunt Laura shook her head. "I didn't even know it was bleeding until you noticed it. How does it look?"

"I can't really tell." Elaine shrugged. "The stitches still look like they're all in place, but I wouldn't think is should bleed after all this time. I think maybe it's infected."

"You called the doctor's office?"

Elaine nodded. "They were already closed, but Dr. Wendall was on his way home and he said he'd stop by and take a look at it." As if on cue a car door slammed outside. "I bet that's him now." Elaine rose.

Dr. Wendall strode purposefully toward the front door. He didn't have his white lab coat on, but he did carry a black doctor's bag. Elaine pressed her lips together and grinned at the sight, pushing the door open so he could come inside.

"Nice bag." She murmured, unable to help herself,

even though she didn't quite feel like she knew him well enough yet to tease him.

He answered her amused grin with a charming one of his own, then turned his attention to Laura.

"Miss Laura, what happened?" Dr. Wendall went down on his knees to examine the deep "v" shaped laceration.

"I am so sorry to impose, Doctor," Aunt Laura said. "I don't know what I did. I must have bumped or scraped it on something, but I don't remember doing it. I didn't think it merited a trip to the emergency room—especially since we're having company for dinner, but Elaine insisted that you look at it."

"Better safe, than sorry." Dr. Wendall gently peeled away the cloth covering the wound on her shin. "Especially since it's Friday and the office would be closed all weekend."

"Still, I hate to trouble you."

Dr. Wendall put one of his hands over Aunt Laura's. "It's no trouble. I'm glad to have a look at it."

Elaine knelt on the other side and watched the doctor's examination. He had a nice way about him. His hands were gentle as they touched and prodded her wound; his voice, soothing when he assured her that she wasn't an imposition.

At length, he finished assessing the injury and looked up. His eyes were the same shade of green that Richard's had been. The exact same shade. Her heart made a small lurch toward him.

"How does it look?" She glanced down.

"It looks infected." He sat on the sofa beside Laura. "I'll call a prescription in for you before the pharmacy closes. You get started taking that this weekend, and then come to the office on Monday."

Dr. Wendall shifted his gaze back to Elaine.

She carefully avoided making eye contact with him. "I should call Lorraine and Justin and tell them we'll have to postpone our dinner."

"Nonsense!" Aunt Laura proclaimed. "Dr. Wendall, is there any reason I can't have my dinner plans go on as intended?"

"No, Miss Laura." He pulled a gauze pad out of his little black bag and ripped open the package. "I see no reason why you can't have your company like you planned." He glanced at Elaine with a wily grin. "You just need to stay off your feet and let Elaine take care of all the work."

"There, now!" Laura beamed. "You see. Everything's all finished and ready, anyway. We'll just have to get it to the table."

"You mean Elaine will have to get it to the table." He corrected her with a grin, not looking up as he continued to put the fresh dressing on her injury.

"Yes. And you'll stay and have dinner with us. Won't you Dr. Wendall?"

"Oh, no, I couldn't—"

"You have other plans?"

"Well...no, I—"

"Then, you can."

He shot a questioning glance at Elaine, but she had no intention of helping him out. She raised her eyebrows and waited for his answer.

He seemed to take that as a challenge. "I'd be delighted."

∂∞⊂

"Thank you all for coming!" Aunt Laura nearly

gushed. "It's so nice to have you here!"

Elaine tried to control her grin as she helped push Aunt Laura's chair under the dining room table. Her aunt loved to entertain. She'd spent a week planning this dinner for Justin, who probably would have been equally happy if they'd simply ordered pizza at the last minute.

"Justin, you're the guest of honor. You sit here across from me so I can tell you again how much I appreciate your help with the porch."

"There's no need to make such a fuss." Justin cast a glance at her and grinned before doing as he was told. "It took me longer than it should have."

"Nonsense! You can't control the weather. And you did way more than we agreed to anyway. The swing was a particularly nice surprise." Aunt Laura patted his hand. "Elaine, you sit there next to Justin.

"And Dr. Wendall, who went above and beyond his Hippocratic Oath and made a house call to check on me when I needed him, you sit there on the other side of Elaine. It's a little chilly for a cookout on our lovely new back porch. So, until spring, this little barbeque dinner will have to do to honor all of Justin's hard work and generosity."

Elaine cast another glance at Justin. *He was blushing!* She couldn't stifle her smile. She'd forgotten the tendency he had to blush at the slightest attention. He'd always been so easy to tease. Oh, and she'd teased him mercilessly a time or two. How nice that something about him hadn't changed.

He glanced up from his plate and looked at her.

"Is it hot in here, Justin?" she whispered. "Should I open a window?"

His blush brightened.

She bit her lip and glanced at her aunt who had offered one of her hands to Lorraine beside her, and the other across the table to Justin.

"Justin, will you say the blessing?" Aunt Laura bowed her head before he could respond.

Elaine looked down at the empty plate, and then in Justin's direction. He offered his hand to her expectantly. And so did Dr. Wendall on her other side.

The giggle she'd been suppressing died in her throat, clobbered by the unexpected hammering of her heart. Slowly, Elaine stretched out her arms, lightly resting her fingers on the upturned palms of both men.

Dr. Wendall's hand closed around hers first, the smooth warmth of his skin sending a current of sensation—like something from her past rediscovered. All she could think of was Richard and the day she met him, the day she knew she loved him.

A second later Justin's fingers closed around hers, as familiar as a best friend's, and she felt rather than saw him bow his head and close his eyes.

She should've closed her eyes for the prayer. But her gaze was riveted to the large, rough-skinned hand that held onto hers. She swallowed, feeling heat creep up her face.

Justin's voice was soft and reverent. Elaine let her eyes drift closed, listening to the soothing sound of it, and letting the warmth of his hand spread until it encompassed not just her hand, but her heart as well.

Had she ever felt this way around him before? Was it even him stirring these feelings, or was it Boyd Wendall? She looked at the doctor's hand. It was clean and smooth, his touch light and intriguing and new.

She'd touched Justin plenty of times: she'd held his hand during a prayer like this, he'd drape a friendly arm around her shoulders. Never had it caused such a swell of...whatever this emotion was. *Infatuation?* No, it couldn't be. Not with Justin.

It was probably this place. Being back here again after so many years. The almost overwhelming temptation to put certain things behind her and start over. It wasn't right. It didn't feel right. But it did feel good.

"Amen."

The solemnly spoken word carried Elaine back to the present. She drew her hands back to her lap and glanced surreptitiously at the faces of those across the table.

A faint smile touched Aunt Laura's lips, like this was all part of a plan.

Mrs. Barnet's lips were pressed together into a grim little line. *Not pleased.*

Victor just looked happy to be there.

She couldn't bring herself to look at Dr. Wendall. Or Justin.

"Can I get you something, Elaine?" Justin gave her a gentle nudge with his elbow. "Maybe a little more ice for your tea?"

She almost gasped. *Was he teasing her back? So confidently?*

Oh, he *had* changed after all.

❧

"Thank you, again, Dr. Wendall—" Elaine pulled the front door closed as she stepped out behind him onto the front porch.

He held up a hand. "There's absolutely no need to thank me at all, let alone again. And please, call me

Boyd."

She smiled and looked down. "Boyd."

A burst of laughter sounded from the house, and she cringed inside, wondering what they must be finding so funny. Certainly not this situation. Not Mrs. Barnet anyway. She looked a bit annoyed at the doctor's—at Boyd's—presence this evening. And Justin had been quiet. Of course, that might not be unusual for him anymore.

Boyd cleared his throat. "So, you're settling in well?"

"Yes." She nodded and looked into those eyes, so like Richard's. He was tall like Richard, too. Over six feet. But his hair was sandy brown and wavy, rather than blond and straight.

"See..." He started. "There it is again."

He'd said it with such an unexpected intensity that she nearly took a step back. "What?"

"Just a moment there when you looked at me..." He paused. "It happened inside, too. Before dinner. You looked at me like...like..." He trailed off and shook his head, then smiled ruefully.

Elaine's answering smile felt a little sad.

"I'd like to see you, Elaine. Personally."

"Boyd, I—"

"I've heard about your story, and I understand your hesitancy. But maybe we could just meet for coffee. Not even a date. Just coffee. On a Saturday morning. Tomorrow."

She shook her head and took a step back, but he reached out and snagged her hand.

"You know, Elaine, I've lived here about four years now. And I've got to tell you, it's been hard to make friends. It's a small town, everybody knows everybody already. They're a little suspicious of outsiders like me."

She gave a little snort of a laugh. "You seem to be doing just fine, Doctor."

"I know, I know." He smiled. At least he was a good-humored martyr. "It looks that way now. But I've spent four long, lonely years working long, lonely hours to build up my practice. And now that it's doing well, I look around and find that I don't have a whole lot of friends. I'm the doctor. I'm a friend when you're sick or injured, but folks just haven't let me in. Their circles of friends are already complete. This is the first dinner invitation I've had."

"No," she drawled as he stepped closer and clasped her hand more firmly. "I don't believe it." *A handsome doctor like you?* It was on the tip of her tongue to say it, but she stopped. He was clearly pursuing her and she didn't want to encourage him unduly.

His pitiful expression was tempered with a slight grin. He was pouring it on good. He *had* been rather insistent that she call him by his first name. And whenever she saw him, he was always alone. So maybe there was more than a grain of truth to what he said.

And she'd been there—new in town, unable or unwilling to make friends. Lonely.

He seemed to sense when she softened. "Just coffee." He said, leaning toward her a little. "Maybe a little brunch, but only if you're hungry."

She relented with a nod and a smile. "Tomorrow."

His grin widened into a full, easy smile. "Tomorrow."

This job was done.

Justin ran one hand over a new post which supported the old porch roof. It hadn't brought in any income. But it had given him a reason to get up and get going in the morning. Even if Laura wasn't able to pay him, it felt good to have a sense of purpose, if only for a few weeks.

So, now what? Back to waiting by the phone for some contractor to call? Back to waiting for someone to respond to one of his ads? Back to sitting alone in that run down old mobile home while Elaine was here? So close.

He blew out a breath and tucked his hands next to his body to protect them from the chill. Work would pick up again when the weather warmed up. At least that's what everyone kept telling him. But until it did he'd have to find a way to fill his days so that he wasn't constantly thinking about her.

He ran a hand over the new porch railing he'd built, and suppressed a bitter laugh. For all that had changed in his life these past few years, he still loved her. And now that she was back he had less to offer her than ever. And now there was Boyd Wendall, out there on the front porch with her right now. Saying *good night*.

"Nice work."

He jumped at the sound of her voice behind him.

"Sorry." She murmured. "Didn't mean to startle you."

He turned around and shook his head. "I didn't hear you come out."

Elaine crossed the porch and took a seat on the swing. "You know, this really is a nice touch."

Justin leaned back against the porch railing as she

settled in and wrapped an old quilt around her shoulders. "I thought you might like it. I remember how much you used to enjoy the one on your front porch when you were a kid, and then the one at the parsonage."

She looked down and was silent for a long moment. "You shouldn't have gone to the extra trouble or expense." Her voice sounded hoarse. She cleared her throat. "But, thank you. I know I'll enjoy it while I'm here."

"Well..." Justin glanced away. She was probably thinking about that old swing now, and all the chilly evenings she'd sat on it with Richard, the two of them wrapped up in a blanket. "It was no trouble. No expense either. It was stored in our barn. I just cleaned it up a little."

Elaine sniffed and dabbed at the corner of one eye. "It's very nice."

He'd made her cry. Justin stifled a contrite groan. What kind of idiot was he? As he'd cleaned and hung the swing he hadn't thought about the memories it might dredge up, only that she'd always enjoyed her porch swing, and now maybe she would again. Maybe if he helped a little to make this place feel more like home she'd be inclined to stay, and possibly let him sit out here with her once in awhile. He expelled a sorry breath and looked down.

Well, he couldn't just stand here and let her cry. He cleared his throat. "So, where's everyone else?"

She sniffed again and looked up, obviously blinking tears away. "Inside looking at Aunt Laura's scrapbook. That's what she's been doing with all her time off her feet." She grinned through the trace of tears. "When I cleaned out that room where she's sleeping now I must have found twenty shoe boxes full of pictures."

He nodded. This was better. A good change of subject, and a smile. It looked a little forced, but at least she was trying.

"Do you know where I might find a job in this town?"

"You need a job?" This was promising. A job meant she was planning on staying longer than he'd suspected. He'd have to do some checking. "I can't think of any place right off hand. But I'll keep an ear open."

"Thanks." Elaine nodded. "If I could just find a job waiting tables, that'd be enough. And we could probably even pay you to do some more work around here. Help fix this place up a little. Get it ready to sell, like we talked about."

Justin shifted his weight. "I could use the work." But how he felt about helping her get this place in saleable condition was another story.

Elaine pulled her feet up onto the swing and tucked the quilt around them. "You did a great job on this porch. Thanks for doing it. It was very kind of you."

Justin nodded. "Y'all are like family. I was glad to do it."

She bit her lip and looked down.

"Justin...?" She stalled, took a breath, and held it for a long time.

He held his breath, too.

Prison. That's what she wanted to know about, he could tell by the tone of her voice. It was bound to come up sooner or later, and there was no way she could possibly not know someone's interpretation of the story. And the strain between them was easing as their friendship resumed. Her wanting to know was natural.

She finally sighed and glanced back at him. "What happened?"

He let his breath out, too, and watched the little cloud of steam it created evaporate. He hung his head and gave it a shake. He wanted her to know his side of the story even though he didn't know how to begin telling it. But he really didn't want to talk about it. Neither did he want her pity. He just wanted it all to be over. He glanced back at her and she spread the quilt open with one arm.

"Come sit down. It's cold."

The breath caught in his chest. Whatever she'd heard, whatever conclusions she'd drawn about him, she trusted him now. She trusted him enough to invite him to sit close and tell her about it. Elaine curled up into a ball and wrapped the quilt around her.

"Come on." she said. "Before the blanket gets cold."

Since she'd been back he thought about how rumors of his incarceration might have affected her perception of him. He'd been faced with the hard reality that it *had* changed her perception of him the night of Laura's accident, when they'd gone to get dinner together. Right before she got into his pickup she'd stopped and looked at him, for a short second, like she didn't know who he was. That's when he'd known that someone had told her something.

She patted the seat.

"I guess you've heard the whole story, then?" He sat down, able to maintain eye contact for a second before shame oppressed him. He put the toe of his boot to the porch to set the swing in motion.

Elaine shook her head. "I'm sure I haven't heard the *whole* story. But I've heard Aunt Laura's take on it."

"I didn't do anything wrong." The words came out so softly they could have been a whisper. *Yeah, you all say that, don't you...*The words echoed through his mind as an ache rose in his throat. He took a deep breath to tamp down the emotion she didn't need to see.

Elaine leaned toward him and covered his hand with hers. "I never believed you did."

Relief surged through him, unexpected and intense, at the knowledge that someone believed in his innocence simply because he said it was so. "The stuff they found...It wasn't mine. I don't know where it came from. I don't know who put it there. I mean, I have my suspicions, but no proof."

Her fingers tightened around his hand. "Who do you suspect?"

Junior Sadler. Their classmate back in school. He'd grown up to be a drunken wannabe rodeo cowboy, always looking for trouble. That's who he suspected, for a number of reasons, not the least of which were the half-dozen times he'd personally arrested Junior. Twice, or maybe more, in front of some woman he'd been trying to impress. But Junior had hated him since they'd been kids. Justin took a breath and looked down at Elaine's hand. She still wore her wedding band.

He pulled his hand away and shook his head. "It doesn't matter. It's done." He tried to swallow down the unrelenting ache at the back of his throat. "I just wanted you to know...I just wanted to tell you for myself that I really was innocent. I know it's hard to believe—an innocent man going to prison. But in my case it's true."

What else was there to say? No need to share the humiliating details of police searching his house while he sat waiting, already a suspect in his own home. No need to relive his arrest; being handcuffed and escorted to a squad car in front of his neighbors, being processed like a criminal, having no visitors but his mother and court appointed attorney, living in a prison dorm for a year, existing in some strange state of shock for at least half that time.

No. He'd said enough. Justin stood. "I should probably be heading home now. It's late."

Elaine drew her hand back under the quilt. "Justin, what about you and Ed?"

"Aw, we're OK. He did everything he could. He stood by me as long as he could. But in the end he didn't believe...He had to do his job. Things are just awkward between us. It's hard seeing him around, you know?"

She nodded, but her brow furrowed.

She didn't know. She'd been through a lot of heartache of her own. Probably more than him. But she didn't understand the unjustified shame he felt. She couldn't. "I should get going."

She reached out and grabbed his hand again before he could pass her. "Justin, I'm sorry."

He squeezed her hand gently. "I wish you had been here, Elaine. I could have used a friend."

7

Elaine wiped away a circle on the mirror, then braced herself with both hands on the bathroom counter. The urge to break down sobbing nearly overcame her, but she fought it. Strange that she should fight the emotion so hard even here, where she was completely alone. She looked up into the mirror and examined her red rimmed eyes.

What had happened to her? She leaned closer to the mirror. When had she started to look so worn down? She may not have been a spectacular beauty when she was a girl. But at least she'd been pretty. When had that changed?

Elaine stood up straight and stretched. All this lack of sleep wasn't helping either. She tousled wet hair with her fingertips. It seemed stupid, in the light of day, to be afraid of a dream. But she'd tried to keep herself awake last night anyway, first by watching television until midnight downstairs, then by reading in bed—not a brilliant idea. She'd startled herself awake with a cry at three a.m., the book lying on her chest, open to the same page she'd started with.

"Oh, Richard." She closed her eyes and whispered his name to the mirror, tears welling again at the recalled images of the dream. But no. She sniffed and opened her eyes. He was gone. She pulled on jeans and a shirt. It was Monday—a new week, a new start. Time to face the day, and get out there to find a job.

When she made it downstairs to the kitchen she nearly tripped over Justin as she rounded the corner. He was down on both knees peeling back the loose portion of the vinyl floor where the radiator had leaked.

"Been leaking awhile, has it?" Justin looked up at her. "Morning, Elaine."

"Morning." She smiled, enjoying the soft sense of comfort his presence gave, and how some of her anxiety lifted just by hearing his voice. "That's what the plumber tells us."

He used a screwdriver to poke at the wood underneath the vinyl. "You've got good hardwood under here, Miss Laura. What made you decide to cover it up?"

"Guess I felt like a change." Aunt Laura winced as she pushed up out of the chair and reached for a plate.

"Here, let me get that for you." Elaine reached the plate first. "You should sit down and take it easy."

"Oh, nonsense!" But she sat back down anyway, looking a bit relieved. "Dr. Wendall says I'm doing just fine."

Elaine rinsed Aunt Laura's and Justin's plates in the sink. "That is *not* what Dr. Wendall said. He said you're progressing nicely, but you're not good as new yet."

"He's only saying that so *you* have to keep bringing me to his office every week."

"Why would he need to do that?" Justin's voice rose quietly from the corner where he worked.

Elaine glanced over at him, but he didn't look up.

He kept peeling away at the vinyl. "The way I hear it, Dr. Wendall has progressed to seeing Elaine outside the office now."

"The way you *hear it*?" She glanced from Justin's back to Aunt Laura, whose eyebrows rose to a startling degree.

"What's this?" Aunt Laura asked, her tone intensely inquisitive.

"Had you not heard, Miss Laura?" Justin continued, not missing a beat. "Elaine and Dr. Wendall met for coffee Saturday morning."

Elaine stood there and blinked. Justin hadn't sounded anything but informative, but the way he'd said *Dr. Wendall* had her thinking he was really more than a little annoyed.

He still had feelings for her. Realization dawned gently. *And he was jealous.* She felt a smile tug at her lips as she pressed a hand to her stomach to settle all the quivery little butterflies that had suddenly been shaken loose.

She glanced at her aunt, whose eyebrows had risen even further, if that was possible, as she assessed her niece's response. *Oh, no!* Aunt Laura had misunderstood. She was thinking that Elaine's reaction was all about Boyd. But it wasn't.

"You told me you had some grocery shopping to do!"

Elaine stammered. "I...I did..." She took a breath, preparing to defend herself, to say that her meeting with Boyd was merely friendly, nothing more. But a knock on the back door interrupted before she could correct anyone's assumption that it was otherwise.

She crossed to the door and opened it to find Ed Lacey inspecting their new back porch by stamping one foot on it.

"Howdy, Elaine."

"Well, good mornin', Ed." Laura was the first to speak from inside the house. "What brings you here this morning?"

"I thought I'd come check on you, Miss Laura. See how you were getting along." Ed stepped inside, completely filling the kitchen with his presence, minimizing the effect only slightly when he removed his dark brown felt Stetson. "Mornin', Justin."

"Ed." Justin sounded surprisingly congenial compared to the way he'd addressed Ed last time she'd seen them together—or rather the way he hadn't addressed him.

"You're looking well. I see you've got some color back in your cheeks." Ed shifted his gaze to Laura.

"I'm getting there. I still spend most of the day either in the recliner or right here, and I still have to take my pain pills every so often. But generally, I feel pretty fit considering."

"Glad to hear it." Ed cast a glance at Justin before returning his attention to Laura again.

What was that look they exchanged? Like they were in cahoots about something. Elaine stared at Justin. If she stared at him long enough he'd surely give something away. He usually did. But he just looked down.

"Is there anything you need?"

"Oh, no." Aunt Laura shook her head. "Elaine takes good care of me."

Ed turned his glance to her. "Actually, another reason I stopped by was because I thought I might have a word with you, Elaine. In private, if you don't mind."

"Um...I..." Elaine stammered a bit before she could stop herself. "Sure. Cup of coffee?"

Ed shook his head. "No, thanks."

She turned and led him into the living room. "Would you like to sit down?"

"No. I only need a minute," he said. "Justin tells me you're looking for a job."

So *that* was it. "Well, yes, I could use a job."

"I could use someone around the office." He continued quickly. "Answering phones, typing, filing—clerical work. Esperanza left in December and I haven't gotten around to replacing her. When Justin said you needed a job I thought I'd give you first crack at it if you're interested."

Elaine looked down, torn between gratitude to this man, who was an old and true friend to her family, and irritation that he hadn't done more to see that Justin's innocence was proven. She swallowed and took a deep breath. "Um...Thank you, Ed. Thanks for thinking of me. But I'm looking for something temporary. Just for a few months. For some extra cash. Nothing long term."

He nodded. "I understand. And I do need someone long term. But listen, you give it some thought. If you decided you might want something more permanent then come on down to the department and we'll get the paperwork started."

"Thanks." She nodded.

"Well, let me know in the next month or so. Otherwise, I'll have to advertise the opening. The office is getting pretty disorganized."

He gave a final nod and turned to go. She followed him back to the kitchen.

"You be sure to give me a call if there's anything you need, Laura." Ed directed a brief nod toward Aunt Laura, put his hat back on, then pulled the door closed behind him.

The room was quiet except for the sound of his boot-clad steps on the porch, then down the stairs, then total silence.

"Well?" Aunt Laura's voice broke it.

Elaine turned to face her. Aunt Laura leaned forward on the table, an expression of delighted anticipation covering her face.

Justin turned back to his examination of the floor, as if he didn't need to know what Ed's visit had been about.

"Well," Elaine began. "It seems *somebody* told Ed that I'm looking for a job."

"Oh!" Laura beamed. "What a morning this has been!"

She glanced at Justin again. He didn't look up. "He offered me Esperanza's job."

Aunt Laura pushed up out of her chair and reached for her cane. "What did you say?"

"I didn't give him an answer." Elaine took a seat at the table and buttered a biscuit then spread a good sized serving of her aunt's red plum preserves on it. An odd sense of satisfaction warmed her when Justin finally did look at her. "He told me to consider it and get back with him."

"I think I need to sit in a more comfortable chair for awhile. Maybe watch a game show or somethin'." Laura turned to go. "Working for Ed sure sounds like it would beat waiting tables."

That it did. It sounded a whole lot better than waiting tables. It also sounded permanent. And how would it make Justin feel, her taking a job at the Sheriff's Office after he'd lost his the way he had. But then, *he'd* told Ed she was looking for something.

Would he be insulted if she turned the job down after he went to the trouble to get her the chance?

The rhythmic beat of Aunt Laura's cane on the hall floor subsided. Then the soft sound of the television drifted in from the living room. She raised her gaze to Justin's face to find him studying her.

"You asked if I knew of any jobs." He sounded defensive. "I didn't think about it the night you asked, but Esperanza left back before Christmas. I didn't know if Ed would be able to replace her, so I just mentioned to him you were looking."

"I didn't realize the two of you were on speaking terms." Elaine popped the last bite of biscuit into her mouth.

He shrugged. "We don't talk much. But if there's something to say I don't have a problem saying it." He turned back to his work, grabbing a hammer and using the claw end to pry loose a section of baseboard. "Besides, I know waiting tables has to be hard work, hard on your feet and back. Doing secretarial work for Ed'll be easier. It'll probably pay better and the hours will be better...You'll get insurance benefits, regular vacation, sick days..."

Elaine smiled. The urge to wrap her arms around him was so strong she almost acted on it. She bit her lip and rose to clear the table instead. He was still such a good friend. Time and circumstances hadn't changed him as much as she'd thought the night of Aunt Laura's Christmas party. Not really. Maybe his defenses against her had just relaxed. He was smiling again. Maybe not as freely as when he was younger. He may not have opened his heart to her yet, but he at least considered the possibility. He minded that she'd had coffee with Boyd. And if he didn't still feel something for her he wouldn't have cared.

Elaine carried her dishes to the sink. "So, um..." She turned and leaned back against the kitchen counter. "My working for Ed wouldn't bother you?"

Justin stopped tugging at the baseboard. He sat still for a long moment as if she'd just said something shocking. Then, slowly, he turned to look at her. "Does it matter?"

She bit her lip again. "We're friends, right?"

He looked down at the hammer in his hand and nodded. "Right. Friends. Which is why it wouldn't bother me." He turned around and resumed work with the baseboard. "You know, if you sanded and refinished this floor it would probably look really good. We'd have to pull up all this vinyl first and see what kind of shape it's in. But I guess we'll need to pull it all up either way."

"Thank you, Justin."

He stopped his work at her soft reply, but didn't say anything. He only nodded.

❧❦

Elaine shivered, pulled her jacket closer and braced against the blustery wind as she walked the short distance from her car to the back door. All her leg work in search of a job to get them through the next couple of months had come to nothing. Prickly Pear wasn't hiring. Neither were the two convenience stores. The Truck Stop had a couple of openings, but even with her experience, she was pretty sure she wouldn't be getting on there.

She pushed the back door open and stepped inside. The manager just had to ask if she had a tighter pair of jeans. "Give the truckers a reason to stop here," he'd said.

She'd fired back before she could stop herself. "As opposed to, say, serving decent food? Or offering clean restrooms?" Not the thing to say to the hiring manager when one really needed a job.

The savory aroma of pizza lifted her spirits. She followed it through the kitchen and into the dining room.

"What's the occasion?" She glanced from Aunt Laura to Justin where they sat at the dining room table with a box of pizza opened between them.

"Elaine! Come join us." Aunt Laura waved her in. "Justin fixed that leaky downstairs shower. He wouldn't take a check, so I offered him lunch instead. Grab a new pack of napkins before you sit down, dear. They're in that bottom drawer there. How did the job search go?"

"Not well." Elaine turned to the sideboard and pulled out the bottom drawer. There were the napkins, just on top of a stack of china—a different pattern than was displayed in the hutch. "How many sets of china do you have?"

"Oh, let's see, there's Mother's, and Granny's in here. Then I have the set that Garden Club raffled off— I won that one—it's up in that old apartment above the garage...."

"Maybe we should have a garage *sale*." Elaine grinned at Justin and dropped the package of napkins on the table. "Then I wouldn't need to find a job quite so urgently."

Aunt Laura didn't respond. She just sort of sat there as if in her own little world for a moment. "Oh." She seemed to come to again "I could never sell this stuff. Too many memories. Speaking of which...I want to show you the scrapbook I've been working on."

Aunt Laura took up her cane and hobbled out of the room.

"I thought the Truck Stop was hiring." Justin reached for another slice of pizza as Elaine took the seat next to him.

"The manager and I didn't hit it off."

Justin nodded and swallowed. "Given any more thought to Ed's offer?"

She sighed. Maybe she'd sabotaged her own chances at the Truck Stop. She'd worked for creepy managers before. It's not like there weren't plenty out there. She glanced over at him. He still had that one eyebrow raised. He'd said it wouldn't bother him. But it would bother her to leave Ed in a lurch when she left in the spring. Two months or so, that's as long as she planned to stay. Hardly enough time for Ed to even train her thoroughly for a new job. Still, she'd given it plenty of thought. She nodded slowly.

The eyebrow dropped. "Good. It's a better job."

Elaine leaned back in the chair as Aunt Laura set the scrapbook on the table in front of her and opened it to page one.

"These are pictures of your mother," Laura said softly. "I know they won't be the same as all the ones you lost in the tornado. But I thought you'd like to have them."

Elaine leaned a little closer to the book. The first photograph, a black and white portrait of a light haired baby girl in a frilly little dress, nearly took her breath away.

She'd had a copy of that one in a scrapbook of her mother's, which she'd inherited. She felt an absent smile form as she ran one finger over a picture of her mom as an infant. A page later there were pictures of a bright eyed little girl in bobby socks. The years progressed as she turned the pages. Her mother went to school, went to camp, took a trip to the Grand Canyon, met her future husband. Then she got married and the photos took on all the color of a new stage of life. Elaine was born and sent home wrapped up in a snug white afghan.

"This is great, Aunt Laura." Elaine had to swallow past the catch in her voice. She cast a glance at her aunt. "I didn't realize you had so many pictures of us."

She felt Justin lean closer to have a look at the album.

"Well," Laura drawled. "When you don't have children of your own, you tend to live vicariously."

"Oh, look, Justin, there's even a picture of your folks." Elaine pointed to the page she'd just turned. There was a picture of Elaine's and Justin's parents, along with some others, sitting at a table on the church lawn.

Justin leaned closer still, until his shoulder touched hers. "Sure is." He gave a soft, low chuckle so close to her ear that she felt it, then he pointed to the bottom corner of the same page. It was a picture of the two of them together. Elaine smiled. They couldn't have been more than eight or nine years old, and each one had an arm draped casually around the other's shoulders. She had been slightly taller than he, and she had her head cocked a little to one side. She was either winking at the camera or squinting against the sun. But Justin's eyes were fixed on her. Even then, at no more than nine years old, he wore an expression of complete devotion.

Elaine looked up at the man who sat so close to her now. The lines of his face were firmer, more mature, but the expression there was remarkably similar. He still smiled from the memory that the picture had recalled and he studied her face for a long moment, his gaze finally coming to rest on her mouth. He swallowed and looked back down at the photo album, but she could tell he wasn't even seeing it anymore.

He wanted to kiss her.

She wanted to let him.

She returned her gaze to the picture book on the table and turned the next pages to reveal the rest of her life with her parents. There was a picture of her and her mother at Astroworld, a picture of her and her father at a local park. There was another in the front hall of their home with Elaine all dressed up and ready for her prom. There was a picture of her and both her parents at her high school graduation, then helping her move into her dorm room at college.

Then Elaine turned to the last page. It contained a single picture, taken at her wedding in which her parents were both conspicuously absent. They had died when she was in college, in a head on collision with an eighteen wheeler on their way to Dallas to visit her. The weekend she planned to introduce them to Richard. Now all three of them were gone.

She swallowed past the lump in her throat and closed the book. Justin had replaced the distance between them by sliding his chair back to its original position.

"Thank you, Aunt Laura." Elaine took a deep breath. "It's a precious gift. I hadn't realized how much I missed my pictures." Not just her pictures. She'd lost everything in that storm, and probably more than she would have if she hadn't just walked away from the remains of it. There had to have been something left, even if it had been strewn all over most of five or ten acres. But she'd just left it there. And now it was reduced to one box in an upstairs closet. Well, it was something.

"Elaine, I've been thinking." Aunt Laura leaned forward in her chair. "And I think I've decided how we can earn a little more income around here."

She forced a grin. "You've reconsidered the garage sale idea?"

"Maybe we could rent out that old garage apartment out back."

No. Bad idea. Not just a bad idea, but an indescribably terrible idea. It sounded like a long term solution when what they needed was just the opposite. Elaine opened her mouth to object, but her aunt seemed to sense her resistance, and turned to Justin.

"What do you think of the idea, Justin?"

He shrugged and then drank the last of his Coke. "I guess it's a fine idea, if you don't mind a stranger living back there."

"Well, of course, it couldn't be just anyone." Laura pulled the photo album toward her and began flipping through its pages again.

"No it couldn't be just anyone." Elaine reached for a slice of pizza. "It shouldn't be anyone at all. I thought the plan was to get this house ready to sell. Won't it be harder to sell if we've got a renter living out back? Is that old apartment even fit to live in?"

"Maybe Justin could have a look at it for us. It may need a little work, but it seems like it would eventually pay for itself. Don't you think?"

"*Eventually?* Eventually neither one of us will live here anymore." She sat back and shook her head. "I...I don't know, Aunt Laura. It seems like a lot of trouble, not to mention up-front expense."

"Just give it some thought, hmm?" Laura rose and took up her cane. She dropped a light hand on her shoulder and held it for a moment.

Elaine sighed, nodded, and cast a glance at Justin.

Aunt Laura gave her shoulder a final pat, and left the room.

Justin shrugged at her. "It's probably not a bad idea."

She took a bite of her pizza and shook her head. It *was* a bad idea. It was just one more thing to spend money on. Money they didn't have. And it sure made it seem like Aunt Laura wasn't quite as eager to sell this place and settle into a cozy little senior citizens' apartment complex as she seemed to be a month ago.

8

Elaine frowned into the vanity mirror on the back side of the sun visor and ran a hand through her hair, trying in vain to smooth it behind her ears. It flipped and curled up at the ends regardless of the pomade she used to try to control it. She looked so shaggy, people here might think she'd gone off the deep end, with her wild hair and the dark circles under her eyes that no amount of makeup could fully conceal.

"You look lovely, honey."

She cast Aunt Laura a skeptical glance. "Look at my eyebrows. Why didn't you tell me they looked so...you know."

"They look just fine to me."

She examined her aunt's eyebrows. OK, so Aunt Laura couldn't be held responsible for knowing when the time had come for a wax. Elaine sighed and flipped her visor back up again. But she was long overdue for one. When she got her first paycheck she'd treat herself. Maybe Shellie still worked at the beauty shop over on Third Street. Maybe she'd be here at church today.

Church. Elaine looked through her windshield at the unassuming little brick building. Her gut clenched. Aunt Laura had not been able to attend since her accident, and she knew how important church was to her. Still, just the thought of walking into that building again was enough to make her heart pound and her stomach twist into tight knots. She found her one and only consolation in the idea that today couldn't possibly be any worse than Christmas Eve.

That thought sustained her as she stepped out of the car, and then helped her aunt out. *I've done it once. I can do it again.* It became her silent mantra as she followed Aunt Laura up the handicapped ramp to the large double doors. She could do this. She stepped inside.

"Elaine!"

She turned toward the sound of her name.

Doctor Wendall waved and strode purposefully across the foyer in her direction. A man on a mission. "I was hoping I'd see you here today." He took her aunt's hand and shook it, then reached out toward her. "I was hoping you ladies would accompany me to Sunday dinner after the service."

"What a thoughtful invitation, Doctor Wendall." Aunt Laura leaned on her cane and linked an arm through Elaine's. "But we've already got dinner plans with the Barnets at our house. Sort of a celebratory meal before Lorraine and Victor's wedding this week. Why don't you join us?"

"Oh, no." Doctor Wendall shook his head and smiled. "I couldn't intrude."

"No intrusion, dear. You're welcome to come."

"Thank you, Miss Laura, but maybe some other time."

"That would be lovely." Aunt Laura gave his arm a pat. "How about Saturday evening?"

"Saturday?" he echoed.

"Yes. The wedding will be over by then and you

can join us for a nice intimate dinner for three. Excuse me, Doctor, I see someone I need to speak with before the service begins. We'll see you Saturday at six." Aunt Laura crossed the foyer with the aid of her cane, managing to catch up with Dot Lacey before she entered the sanctuary.

"She's a force to be reckoned with." Boyd grinned at Elaine.

"They should name a hurricane after her."

He stepped aside so that she could precede him into the sanctuary. "Saturday at six, then."

Elaine took a deep breath as she entered the space. The past five years of her life seemed to dissolve instantly, leaving her with a surreal feeling that no time had passed since the last Sunday morning service she attended here as the pastor's wife.

Aunt Laura had taken a seat in the family's usual pew, a little more than halfway toward the front on the left, in front of Lorraine, Victor and Justin. Elaine slid in beside her. It felt familiar, if not comfortable, to be here again, in the same seat she'd occupied in her youth with her parents. Then without them, hearing Richard deliver countless sermons. No. She shook her head slightly to herself. Not countless. His time here with her had been so short she probably *could* count them.

She closed her eyes. She could see him emerging from the door in the choir loft to take his place on the platform. On some level she expected him to at any moment, as if the feeling of moments ago was real and no tragedy had happened, no time elapsed.

The door in the choir loft opened and the small choir filed in followed by the music director and the new pastor. Elaine stifled a gasp at the sight of someone other than Richard emerging from that door. It took every ounce of self control she had to contain the tears that rushed to the surface. From the corner of her eye, she saw Laura look over at her.

But then the memories came surging, one after another, like waves. All she could see was Richard at the pulpit delivering the sermon. She closed her eyes and she could hear his voice, that down-home, conversational style of his, underscored by the twang that gave him away as a small town boy the second he spoke.

She could see him sitting in his study in their home, pouring over various Bible translations, dictionaries and commentaries and a slew of reference books that never made it back to the bookshelves unless company was coming.

Images of him bombarded her; of how he would cut the grass on Saturdays while she worked in the flower beds, but not before he helped her cook breakfast so that they could crawl back into bed and eat it there. Suddenly she could remember with cruel clarity every little detail about him; how he smelled after a shower, how the stubble on his face felt against her skin in the morning before he shaved, how warm his skin felt when she touched him, how she always felt when he touched her, kissed her, made love to her.

Then came the images of Ed and Justin standing on her front porch in the pouring rain telling her that there had been an accident. Of his cold, lifeless body being dressed in the funeral home, and then in the casket at the service.

One after another the memories came, until somewhere in the fuzzy and far away present she heard the preacher end his sermon and ask that everyone stand for the invitation. Elaine stood mechanically feeling the pressure of the tears building, like a well, tapped and drilled until it had no choice but to gush. The tears were coming and she could not stop them.

She bolted from her place next to Laura, knowing only that she had to get out of this building, aware of little else but the steps it took to carry her to the front door, outside, across the lawn and down the farm to market road that led to the old parsonage. Elaine walked the quarter mile quickly, gathering control of herself and her emotions, reaching down deep to find the anger that had been her almost constant companion until recently.

The lot stood empty now. She veered off the road and into the vacant field. To her left ran the thickly overgrown ruts that had once been her driveway. No remnant of the house remained. To her right, a few yards away, grass and weeds had overtaken the storm cellar. She pressed a hand to her chest, her anger dissipating in a wave of grief, but she hardened her heart.

No! Elaine sniffed as her grief turned to rage. She would *not* give God the satisfaction of her broken heart. She forced the tears back down to their source and steeled her heart and her mind as tires ground to a stop on the gravel road. She sniffed and turned.

Justin stepped out of his truck. The wind ruffled his hair as he stood watching her for a long moment. Finally he stepped toward her.

She turned back to the empty lot and focused on it as if the sheer force of will could make that house and that life materialize before her once more before Justin convinced her to go.

"Elaine..." His voice was gentle when he said her name. "It's OK to cry about it."

"What difference will it make?" The words came out sounding flat. "It's gone. There's nothing left. Just a few things in a box at Aunt Laura's. It's like it never even existed."

Justin put hands on her shoulders and turned her around to face him. He searched her face for a long moment, then wrapped his arms around her.

The urge to burrow into his arms and cry like a child nearly overwhelmed her. She had been numb to so many things—contentedly so—before returning here and reconnecting with him. But *this*...Standing here in Justin's arms. Being held, being loved by someone. This was the first good thing she'd felt in years. A tear slid down her cheek and she wrapped her arms around him.

"Elaine, you try to be so strong." She buried her face in his neck and listened to the soothing cadence of his voice. "You've always been that way. But you don't have to be. You've lost a lot—everything. And it's OK to cry about it and let your friends take care of you for awhile. So go ahead and cry, or yell, or whatever you need to do. You'll probably feel a lot better."

"I've spent the last five years yelling. At God. It hasn't helped."

"Then yell at me. I can take it."

She squeezed her eyes shut and felt another tear slip down her cheek. He could take it. He could take so much that he didn't deserve. But she didn't want to yell at him. She didn't even want to yell at God anymore. She just wanted to curl up somewhere and disappear. With a shuddering sigh she pulled out of his arms and took a step back. "I don't want to talk about it."

"Maybe not now," he said. "But if you ever do, you know I'll be here for you."

"Thank you, Justin." She reached out and took his hand, giving it a squeeze accompanied by a feeble smile, then she started for his truck, only letting go of his hand when he followed her. When she made it to the road she turned around for another look at the ghostly lot. Not one sign existed that would lead anyone to suspect a home had once stood here. There were only gnarled and leafless mesquites and post oaks in the foreground, and behind them stood a grove of live oaks thriving despite the wintry landscape. Now it was just an empty lot, waiting for someone to come put a house on it and build a life here, to replace the one she had lived with Richard

"I meant what I said." His voice broke the silence. When you're ready to talk about it, or cry, or yell, or scream about it, I'll be around to listen."

"Thanks. But I couldn't ask it of you, Justin. You've always done so much for me, and I..." She let her voice trail off. *I'm not inclined to hang around here forever any more than I was the last time we stood together on this road. I'd leave again this very afternoon if Aunt Laura didn't still need me.*

Finally she raised her gaze to his.

He held it for a moment, as if to make sure she got the point. "I'll still be around."

❧

"So have you heard anything from the newlyweds yet?" Elaine grinned up at Justin before leading him down the back porch steps.

He laughed. "I don't expect I'll hear from them until they get back."

"A Caribbean cruise." She heard the longing in her own voice and chuckled. "Must be nice."

She led him across the distance between the house and the garage. All this week she'd considered Aunt Laura's idea of renting the garage apartment. Her first objection had been hasty. She hadn't wanted to digress from the original plan: sell the house, get Aunt Laura settled into a nice new apartment, and then make a clean break, once and for all. But the more she thought about the garage apartment idea, the more she thought it could work. It would solve the money shortage they had. Aunt Laura wouldn't be here totally alone. It may not be as clean a break as she'd hoped for, but she could leave sooner. And after what happened at church last Sunday, that aspect of this new plan held a lot of appeal. She'd never feel at home here again.

Elaine stopped at the foot of the weathered staircase attached to the side of the garage. Maybe it didn't look exactly rickety. But it was probably nearly as old as the back porch. And look what had happened to *it*. She cast a wary glance up the stairs, then handed Justin the key when he stepped up beside her. "You go first."

"So if the stairs crumble I'll be the one with the broken neck?"

So he was thinking the same thing. "Hey, you're the professional."

Justin grinned at her and took the key, stepping gingerly on the bottom stair, giving a little bounce to test its soundness. Then he took another stair, then another.

"Whoa!" His distressed shout pierced the calm

evening. Before she could react, he collapsed into a heap.

"Justin!" Elaine sprang up the few steps beneath him and dropped to her knees. She clutched the front of his shirt. "Are you OK?" She scanned him thoroughly, looking for blood or protruding bones and, finding none, settled her gaze on his face.

He was grinning. And the stairs were still solid beneath them.

"Oh! You jerk!" The indignation she felt flooded her face in a warm rush. She punched him half heartedly in the chest.

Justin flinched playfully and burst out laughing.

"I thought you'd broken your neck!"

That only made him laugh harder.

Elaine relented and smiled. A series of giggles escaped, paving the way for the laughter that followed. It was funny. The sort of prank he might have pulled when they were younger. She'd fallen for it now just like she would have then.

Her laughter died when his arms closed around her, but she remained breathless. His eyes, blue like the sky on a clear summer day, searched hers intently. The only times she'd seen the lines of his face as relaxed as they were now had been on an occasion or two when he hadn't been aware she watched him. She reached up and brushed a lock of his hair away from his forehead. *What would it feel like to kiss him?* He drew her tentatively closer. *Just one short, sweet, soft kiss.* It had been so long. No man had held her like this, or kissed her since Richard.

Richard.

The thought almost made her gasp. Elaine tore her gaze from Justin's face and pushed herself up off of him. "OK." She cleared the thickness from her throat. "So we know the stairs are still in decent shape."

She stared at her feet, then at the stairs, the door at the top, anywhere but at Justin as he got up and continued up the stairs. Finally she lifted her gaze to the doorknob as he turned the key in the lock and then pushed the door open. She followed him inside the small apartment and flipped on the light switch just inside the door.

"This isn't so bad." Justin picked his way around and through a maze of boxes scattered throughout the small living room.

She hadn't been up in this old apartment since she was a girl, but she could remember losing track of hours up here exploring the family's old treasures. She took a deep breath, inhaling the familiar fragrance of old books and mothballs. Of course she hadn't noticed it back then, but the little place had some charm. The walls were beaded board all around with a warm amber finish. To the right, there was a small kitchenette. Bookshelves lined the far wall, surrounding the door she knew led to the small bedroom and bathroom.

"Looks like you've got a leak there." Elaine glanced back at Justin and followed his pointed finger to a stain on the ceiling. "And there."

"So we'd probably need to start with replacing the roof?" That was good. Or was it bad? Why couldn't she think straight? The roof would be expensive. There was no way they could afford a new roof, even if it was only the garage.

"Maybe this weekend I can climb up there and take a better look. You might not actually need to *replace* it."

He wandered into the kitchen, turned on the faucet and let the water run for a few seconds. Then he squatted down and opened the cabinet under the sink. She dragged her gaze from his back and lifted the lid of a box near her. It was full of books. But she hardly even saw them. A fresh wave of heat rushed to her face. She'd almost kissed him. She ran a hand absently over the cover of an old book, remembering the feel of his chest vibrating with laughter, the warmth of his arms as they'd closed around her.

The air around her stirred with the scent of his cologne as he brushed past her, muttering something about having a look at the bathroom. She squeezed her eyes shut and shook her head. *What am I thinking? It's Justin!* She'd never felt this way about Justin. He was a good man, and a good friend. But this attraction and desire—these were not her feelings for him. Elaine shook her head again, trying to restore her sense of reason. She was lonely. That was all.

And what was up with him? Hadn't they just almost shared a kiss out there? And now here he was, all business, inspecting the place as if nothing had happened.

He really had kissed her once. In the ninth grade.

"Elaine?"

She jumped and spun around as Justin came back out of the bedroom. "Hmm? How does it look?"

"Good." He uttered an astonished sounding chuckle. "Surprisingly good. Do you know if she's got someone in mind to rent this place?"

She glanced back at him and narrowed her eyes. Then she shook her head. "I don't think so. Not really. Why? Do you know someone who might be interested?"

"Um. Yeah." He met her gaze again. "Me."

Elaine nearly choked. "*You* want to live here?"

Justin nodded. "If it's OK. I'll be getting paid pretty regular now and it'd be more convenient to live here in town. I'll still be close enough to my mother to be able to help her and Vic out a little if they need it." He paused and reached up to rub the back of his neck. "Besides, it's time I started to step out on my own again..." His voice trailed off, but he clearly expected some response.

OK, so here was a twist she hadn't anticipated. But it could work.

"What do you think?"

She nodded slowly. Aunt Laura would have her money. Justin would be a little further along in his process of starting over. And she could leave with some measure of peace, if not a totally clear conscience. "Let's go talk to Aunt Laura."

❧❧

He couldn't read her. Justin glanced at Elaine where she leaned back against the kitchen counter, arms folded across her chest, gaze fastened on the floor between her feet. Did she like the idea of him moving in above the garage? Did she hate it? Did she care?

Then there was that moment on the stairs, when his little prank had nearly ended with a kiss. If only it had. Then maybe she'd know how much he still loved her. But in the same moment that he made up his mind to go ahead and kiss her, she'd thought of Richard. He saw it in her eyes. He looked down at the table. Sometimes he'd swear she had feelings for him that went well beyond friendship. Other times, like now, she barely acknowledged his presence in the room.

"I think it's a wonderful idea!" Laura's enthusiastic voice gave him a little jolt. She gave a stir to whatever it was she had cooking on the stove, then put the lid on the pot.

Justin glanced back at Elaine. Nothing. No sign of what she thought.

"Think about it." Laura crossed the kitchen to come sit beside him at the table. "It's perfect. We know him. We trust him. It's a perfect solution!"

"Perfect." Elaine echoed faintly.

Justin shook his head. *No, no, no.* Something wasn't right about this. It was all falling into place too easily. His life didn't work this way anymore. "Listen, if the idea bothers you, I'll understand. It was just a thought, I certainly don't have to—"

"No." Elaine shook her head and finally looked up at him. "Aunt Laura's right. It's a good idea. I mean, who better? We know you. We trust you..." Her voice trailed off and her gaze meandered back to the floor but he could see the wheels turning.

What was she up to? He shoved a hand through his hair, dropped it back to the table, and glanced at Laura. She gave him a wink and a grin.

"So, when can you move in?"

He felt a smile emerge despite his sudden misgivings. It was settled, then. A new place. A nicer place. "Honestly, Miss Laura, I could move in tomorrow if you'd let me."

"Oh, no, dear. We'd have to clean it up some first. Figure out what to do with all those old boxes up there." She leaned a little closer, very conspiratorially. "Maybe we'll have that garage sale Elaine keeps nagging me about."

"It won't bother me to live with it until you can decide what to do with it." He tried to sound accommodating. But really, he couldn't be out of that musty old mobile home fast enough.

"Whatever you decide, dear." Laura gave his hand a pat. "Oh, Elaine, would you put those dinner rolls in the oven for me?"

Elaine slid them into the oven just as a knock sounded on the back door.

"That will be our dinner guest." Laura rose from her chair and went to answer the door.

Elaine turned, her brow creased, but then a look of alarm lit her features. She raised a hand to her hair. Justin shifted in his chair. What was this bad feeling in his gut? Like something was about to go majorly wrong.

"Dr. Wendall, come in." Laura swung the door open to allow their guest entrance.

Elaine's expression had grown even more alarmed as Wendall stepped across the threshold into the house. Through the *back* door, as if he was a regular part of the family now. And he'd brought flowers. Of course.

"Good evening." Wendall said, obviously in high spirits. He handed the flowers to Elaine. She took them with a smile and a soft, sweet thank you for the doctor, and an uneasy glance back at Justin.

She might as well have slapped him. He felt every muscle in his body tense. His hands balled into fists as he pushed his chair back from the table and rose. "I should be going."

"Oh, no. Stay." Laura insisted.

"Justin, wait—" Elaine stepped towards him, reached out to touch him. But he sidestepped her.

"No...thanks. I really need to go. Good night."

He crossed to the back door, opened it, and stepped outside. *Typical.* This was so very typical of her, of his life. Not an hour ago she'd been in his arms, about to kiss him, and now this! Now she was seeing another guy! A doctor, for crying out loud! And what was he? He shook his head. Nothing, compared to that.

His footsteps carried him to his truck as if by their own will.

Fine. He slammed the truck door, shoved the key into the ignition and started the engine. Let her go ahead and date her doctor. She could marry him for all he cared. Maybe then she'd have a reason to stay, since he'd obviously never been enough.

9

"Thank you so much for inviting me to dinner." Boyd pulled the door closed as he stepped out onto the back porch.

"Thank you for coming." Elaine tucked in her sweater to withstand the evening chill, resisting the urge to remind him that it was her aunt who had invited him.

"It's a rare thing for me to say no to a home cooked meal. But I know a great little Chinese place over in Georgetown. Do you like Chinese food?"

"Mmm." She nodded. "Yes. Richard and I had a little place in Dallas we liked to go to, way downtown. It was just a little hole in the wall, but the food was great."

She turned to look out into the dark backyard, at his car, at her car, at anything but him. Finally her gaze landed on the stairs of the garage apartment. About half way up.

"You enjoyed living in Dallas?"

"Yes." She nodded and glanced over with a smile. "Not the traffic. But even that wasn't too big a deal considering all the other great things about being in the city."

"Do you miss it?" Boyd leaned back against the porch railing.

She sighed. *Did she?* Dallas was one of the best

times of her life. She'd been young and in love,
planning her wedding, her future...That's where she'd
lived when her parents passed away, but that was the
only dark spot, and she'd had Richard to help her cope.
They started their life together in Dallas. She glanced
out to the clear sky as if a definitive answer would
come from there. There were never this many stars out
at night in Dallas.

The day of the tornado she'd climbed aboard a bus
bound for Dallas, thinking she'd rather live there than
anywhere else. She had friends there from her college
years. But in the end the memories of her life with
Richard had been too much to bear and she had fled to
San Antonio. No. She could never live in Dallas again.
"I miss that time. You know? It's not so much the place
I miss as the time."

Boyd nodded and looked down at the keys in his
hands. He turned them a couple of times, then shoved
them back into his pocket and studied her face intently.

He was gauging his chances of kissing her,
although she didn't know why. She hadn't given him
any reason to believe that she might welcome such an
advance. His gaze lingered on her face, and something
about his demeanor shifted. All evening he'd been the
picture of confidence and charm, but now he seemed
nervous. He rubbed his hands together and then
dropped them to his sides, taking a small, hesitant step
toward her.

But all she could think about was Justin. She could
still feel the warmth of his arms when he'd held her as
she cried after church last Sunday, and then again just
a few hours ago when he'd pulled that stupid prank,
pretending to fall through the garage stairs. She had to
suppress a smile at the memory. But the urge to grin

subsided at the memory of his devastated expression after Boyd had arrived for dinner.

She took a step backward. "Thanks again for coming, Boyd. We had a nice time. And thank you for the flowers." She went towards the door, but he stopped her with a hand on her arm.

"So, can I see you again?" Boyd's question hooked her before she could get away. She blinked a few times.

"Um..." She bit her bottom lip. "Boyd, I had such a nice time this evening...But I—"

He reached for her hand. "Give me another chance before you say no. I'm a good guy, and I know at least one of my patients who thinks I'd make a good catch."

She matched his grin. No doubt he'd make a good catch. "Are you implying that you want to be caught?"

He chuckled. "See there, I've already said too much." He gave her hand a gentle squeeze. "What do you say? Can I call you? Maybe I could take you to that little Chinese place?"

She glanced into his face. He was so very nice. Quite handsome, with brown hair that curled a little, those green eyes, and a wide, genuine, easy smile. He knew all about her baggage. She couldn't possibly have been fun tonight, as absorbed as she was with thoughts and worries about Justin. Still he wanted to see her again.

She looked back down. "Boyd, I...I don't think...I just can't."

He took a deep breath and let it out evenly. "Is it Justin?"

She raised her gaze to meet his.

"Are you and he..." Boyd's voice trailed off as if he didn't know exactly how to phrase the question.

"Justin and I grew up together. He's probably the

best friend I have."

"But other than that, you're not...*involved*?"

She searched the area around her feet. *Were* they involved? She had her perspective. She was sure he had his. But even in high school, Justin had never asked her out on a real date. Why had he never made that move? Her life might have turned out so differently if he'd only done something about his feelings.

As nice a man as Boyd was, he didn't inspire those little jittery signs of infatuation that she'd had recently around Justin. Boyd didn't dominate her thoughts, wasn't who she really wanted to be with right now. Boyd wasn't the one who had always been there for her, consistent, unchanging.

"Not technically." She sighed and gave what she hoped was an apologetic look. "But yes, on some level, I think we are. It's just that I've been gone so long, and his life is so different now. And I'm more than a little confused by my feelings for him..." She let her voice trail off.

"But you do have feelings for him." His smile faded and he looked disappointed, but not devastated. He nodded, gave her hand a parting squeeze and turned to leave. Halfway across the yard he turned back. "Good night."

"Night." She bit her bottom lip as he continued to his car, then waved as he started the engine and drove away.

She felt her face contort as a completely unexpected sob rose from deep inside. How could she be doing this? Standing here on the front porch after what was technically a date, even if it had occurred unintentionally. It couldn't possibly be right to see one man this way when she had feelings for another. And more wrong still, to have feelings for anyone when she missed Richard so much she could hardly breathe when she thought about him. How could this pain still cut so sharply after five years? It should be better by now, not worse.

But worse it was, almost like she'd never really felt it before.

∂∽

Elaine pushed hands into jacket pockets and glanced up at the cloudless sky. *What am I supposed to say when I get there?* She rolled her eyes and shook her head. Not much use in asking for God's help now, was there?

This last day of February was just about perfect. Not a cloud in sight, crisp and chilly, but not really cold. Too bad she couldn't just enjoy it. She'd traversed most of the quarter mile between Mrs. Barnet's house and Justin's mobile home, thinking the fresh air might clear her head and inspire just the right words that would make things right between them again. But there the trailer stood, just yards away, and the words were no more present than when she'd set out.

She furrowed her brows and felt her heart sag a little more, if that was possible. The trailer was the ugliest shade of yellow she had ever set eyes on, and it looked more decrepit than any place that someone should live. The concrete stoop wobbled a little when she stepped onto it and raised her hand to knock. What *was* she going to say? She shook her head to clear away the uncertainty, then followed through. There wasn't even time to gather thoughts before Justin pulled the door open. He straightened up and took a small step back. His shock couldn't have registered more clearly. She was the last person he'd expected to come knocking on his door.

"We, um...I mean, *I* missed you at church this morning." She dared to glance back at him. His gaze was cold, angry. But he stepped aside and held the door open for her to come in anyway.

Tension emanated as she passed him and stepped inside. He closed the door. She swallowed hard and turned to face him. His form was solid and unmoving between her and the exit. It was about the only thing she could see for a second or two. But the details of the room emerged from the dimness as her eyes adjusted to the different light level, as did the answer to her question regarding whether or not they were involved in any way other than friendship.

Oh, yeah. They were involved. They may not have discussed it at any point. But in his mind, as well as hers, something real had started between them, despite her best efforts to prevent it. And she'd hurt him badly. *Again.*

"I thought I'd take the morning to pack a few things and move them over." The coolness of his tone was appropriately underscored by the chill in the room. Elaine folded arms and looked away, surveying the room, its contents, anything besides him for a moment.

The place was tidy, but so old. And not "been in the family for a hundred years" old, but rather "third-hand, used-up-by-strangers" old. The worn brown carpet was battered and stained. The place had a musty smell and it probably always stayed just as chilly as it felt right now.

It made perfect sense that he'd want to move out.

He reached down and retrieved a box from the floor. Elaine sighed as quietly as she could and looked down. This would be so much easier if he would just let her have it. If he'd yell at her and tell her just how detestable he thought she was. It would make her feel a little more like she was getting what she deserved after all these years. But that wasn't his way. He had a seemingly endless fuse.

"Justin, I didn't know—"

"Your aunt said the furniture up there would stay." He cut her off as he turned his back and crossed the room. "That'll make the move easier. It's better stuff anyway."

She bit her lip. He wouldn't let her explain. At least, not yet. That was all right. She'd bide her time until he was ready.

"Could you use some help?" She forced a light tone. "I could help pack your kitchen."

He reached up to rub the back of his neck, then looked up toward the ceiling. But he didn't turn around to face her. "Do what you want, Elaine."

That's what you always do, anyway. She sensed the thought as clearly as if he'd said it out loud.

She grabbed a box from a pile on the floor and took it to the cramped kitchen. Not a kitchen that saw much use judging from the looks of it.

Justin stood still for a long moment then crossed to the television, squatted down and unhooked the DVD player. A minute later he stood and carried it to a box.

"Justin, if I could just—"

"There's no need to explain anything, Elaine." He wouldn't meet her gaze. "I get it."

"No, you don't—"

Justin held up a hand and shook his head. "You know what, since you're here, there's something of yours I should return to you."

He rose, crossed the room, opened the door and slipped outside before she could scramble out of the kitchen. She hurried to catch up with his long strides across the pasture. When she did, he was swinging open the door of his father's old hay barn. A gust caught the door and blew it completely open, and he bolted it on the outside so it would stay.

He pressed into the dusty half-lit space beyond the open door without so much as a glance behind him to make sure she'd followed. But follow she did, close behind until he found a light switch and turned it on. A fluorescent shop light came on and buzzed like a giant, angry hornet above her head.

She would have smiled if the walk hadn't seemed to aggravate Justin's temper. She hadn't been inside this barn since they used to play hide and seek. There were so many great places to hide on this old farm.

She pressed her lips together. Once, when she was fourteen, he'd kissed her in this barn. It had been on Valentine's Day and her family had come back to his house after a youth banquet at church. While the adults had coffee inside, she and Justin had come outside into the chilly February wind. They'd ended up in here, seated on an old bench and leaning against a wall of hay bales. He hadn't held her hand, touched her face or anything of the sort. He'd simply leaned over and kissed her, softly, hesitantly. Her head swam and her face flushed, something that had never before happened to her in Justin's presence, and she kissed him back. It had been her first kiss, and it had been soft and sweet and wonderful.

She touched fingertips to her mouth and glanced at him. He stood in the middle of the barn, hands on his hips, looking every bit as dour as he had that first night at Aunt Laura's Christmas party.

"Justin, I—"

He shook his head. "Come on." He turned and pressed further into the barn, stopping in a back corner beside an old stack of hay bales and a large mound of something that was covered with an old blue tarp.

Justin paused for a moment, studying the heap in front of him before he moved around to the side and began to pull the tarp off, scattering dirt, dust and hay in every direction. He settled the tarp to the ground, tamping it down with his feet, revealing a mass of boxes in various sizes and conditions, stacked about chest high.

Elaine coughed, then stepped closer. What was this? He said it belonged to her, but she didn't have anything. He opened a smaller box on top of the stack, peered inside and shuffled things around. She pressed a hand to her mouth as the tears began to pool again.

No. He didn't. He hadn't.

He pulled out an oak jewelry box. It had four drawers in the front and a lid that was hinged onto the back. When he opened it, it would have a mirror inside. How many times had she looked into that mirror? Before church on Sunday morning, before going out to dinner with her husband. How many times had she traced the initials that were carved on the lid? *EM—Elaine Mallory.*

Richard had it made for her and had given it to her for their first anniversary.

Elaine closed the distance between her and Justin, ran her hand lightly over the lid, and traced her initials with the tip of her finger. A tear rolled down her cheek and landed on her hand.

She sniffed and pushed the lid open. The mirror was broken, cracked into six or seven fragmented and chipped pieces, but the glue held it fast to the underside of the lid. She could still see the whole thing as it had once been, filled with earrings, rings, necklaces, pins and bracelets, as well as so many other trinkets that her loved ones had given to her through the years. Now it was empty except for the stiff and water stained green velvet fabric that lined it.

Justin pressed the jewelry box into her arms, then he delved back into the box. He lifted out a small plastic bag with a few pieces of jewelry in it.

"I found these, too." Justin handed the bag to her.

Elaine set the jewelry box down on a bale next to her and pulled open the bag. The first thing she pulled out was the tiny opal ring that Richard had given her on their six month anniversary. Another tear fell. She tried to blow some of the dirt out of the setting.

"Where did you find this?" The words were barely more than a whisper.

Justin shrugged. "Don't remember exactly. Near where the house was."

Elaine slipped the ring onto a finger and examined it closely. Such a small little thing, and yet so precious to her. And he had managed to find it in the midst of all the wreckage, knowing, even if she didn't, that one day she'd long to have it back. She couldn't summon sufficient words to thank him.

She reached back into the bag and pulled out the pearl choker that her mother had given her on the morning of her high school graduation day. She swallowed a sob that rose to the surface at the sight of the family heirloom that she had been so quick to leave behind.

Next she pulled out a stick pin topped by a deep purple amethyst set with a small swirling pattern of gold behind it. The pin had also been given to her for her high school graduation—by Justin. She closed her fingers around it and squeezed her eyes shut as the tears began to fall freely.

"Oh, Justin..." She raised her blurry, tearful gaze to his face.

"There's more." His gruffness of only moments ago had dissipated, and his tone now was heartbreakingly tender.

Elaine delved into the box again and came up with her old Bible. Its burgundy leather cover was dry and stiff from its encounter with the elements these past five years. Although the gold had worn off of the lower right corner of the cover where her name was stamped, she could still make out the letters.

Elaine Royden. Her parents had given her the Bible long before she got married and she never did change the name. There hadn't been any room to add Mallory to the end of it. The fact had never bothered Richard, although he offered to buy her a new Bible once. But she'd used this one for years. She had marked where she'd come to some special insight pertaining to its text. To buy a new Bible seemed like starting over.

If only she could.

She pulled open the Bible and flipped through the pages until the book fell open, on its own, to the book of Romans. There a verse was highlighted from years ago, and she read it silently.

...And we rejoice in the hope of the glory of God. Not only so, but we also rejoice in our sufferings, because we

know that suffering produces perseverance; perseverance, character; and character, hope.

She snapped the Bible shut and glanced at Justin who had turned away from her, hands stuffed into the front pockets of his jeans.

What could she possibly have known about suffering when she'd highlighted that passage? Maybe she'd done it after her parents' death, she couldn't remember. But even at that point, her suffering had only begun. And what about perseverance? She'd done enough of that to still be in this world. But that would merely be existence, survival, not perseverance. And character? Hope? No. She had gained none of those.

Years of running away from God will do that to you. She shook the thought from her head and blinked away another round of tears.

She looked back up at Justin. He had suffered, too. He had persevered, through a year in prison for a crime he didn't commit. And no one, even if they believed he had hit a rough patch in his life and made a mistake worthy of prison time, could say he didn't now possess character of the highest quality. And hope. What did he hope for? He had hoped for her return enough to collect all these things and save them for her. And here she was. She closed her eyes as more tears fell.

And what was she that he would care about her in such a way? So faithfully. So unconditionally. She didn't deserve it.

She heard him walk away and she opened her eyes.

"Justin." She swiped at her tears with one hand.

He turned around and met her gaze.

"Thank you."

కొళ

Justin clenched his jaw and kept a steady pace back to his trailer. Much as he wanted to, he couldn't just let it go. Not this time. That near kiss on the steps had proven that she at least felt something for him. She might be lonely and confused, but he was pretty sure there was more to it than that. And he had waited so long for her to come around. He wouldn't stick around through her courtship with the doctor. He wouldn't watch her fall in love with someone else again. He wouldn't be good old dependable Justin anymore.

He charged up the steps, yanked open the door and stepped inside. She'd come out here today to do what she thought she could to make things right between them, to smooth things over. Not to apologize for hurting him. Sure, she might feel badly about it, but only because it meant he was angry with her and might not be around to do whatever she wanted him to do. To give her what she needed.

He felt the muscles in his jaw working. *Dadgum*, he was mad! It took every ounce of self control he had not to hit something. He took a deep breath through his nose and let it out.

But, no. She *had* come out here to apologize. She was sorry she'd hurt him. She'd been sorry every time she'd ever hurt him. But today was different. Something about her today was different. He'd seen it in her eyes. She'd tried to say something but he hadn't let her.

And then he'd taken her out to the barn and shown her all her things.

Why had he done that? Why when he was so angry?

Maybe he wanted her to take her things and go, and let him give up hoping once and for all that she'd come around to loving him like he loved her. Maybe she *would* now that she had them back. A sudden catch in his chest nearly took his breath away. He shook his head and toed at a box on the floor. No. He didn't want her to go. He wanted her to stay. Forever. But not like this, not the way things had always been between them, and that seemed to be the road they'd taken again.

He stepped back to the door and propped one arm up on the jamb. The barn stood wide open. She was in there going through her memories, alone. Maybe he should have stayed with her. But he'd suddenly felt like an intruder as she started to shuffle through the boxes' contents. So many of the things he'd found and salvaged had been Richard's. And it seemed like she was just now starting to grieve.

He'd loved Elaine almost as long as he could remember. It had bothered him every time she'd gone out on a date in high school with someone, but he waited patiently, faithfully, trusting that one day she'd notice him. It broke his heart when he'd heard of her engagement, even though he hadn't seen much of her in the years since she'd left home for college. He'd done OK as long as they lived in Dallas where the thought of her married to another man was just some vague, unrealized idea in his mind. But when they'd moved back here, jealousy had almost eaten him up.

Justin reached up and rubbed his hand across his forehead. Despite the bitterness he felt for the both of them, he and Richard had eventually become friends. They'd meet up for coffee at the Prickly Pear just about every Tuesday morning. Elaine had probably never even known about that. He pushed the hand through his hair and down across the back of his neck. Richard's death had been a big loss to him, too. Bigger than she would probably ever know, especially since the whole accident was his fault.

He tamped down the ache that rose in his throat and expelled a burdened breath. But he could still feel the jealously, as acutely as if it were yesterday. He wouldn't continue down this road again. It stopped here, now, today. Even if it meant *he* ran away from home this time.

10

The golden light of the late afternoon sun stretched deep into the barn through the open door. Elaine closed her eyes, warmed by it where she sat on a bale of hay.

Unbelievable.

But when she opened her eyes she was still here, in Justin's barn, surrounded by all the things he'd salvaged for her, which would have been no small task given the devastation of that storm.

No telling how many days or even weeks he had combed through the rubble just to find the big things. But he'd found CDs and photographs. He'd found tiny pieces of jewelry, and he'd brought them all back here, cleaned them up, boxed them with care and stored them away. What had caused him to hope, after the way she'd left, that she'd ever return? How had he known that one day she'd want all this back? His devotion staggered her.

She took a deep breath and let it out evenly as she could, then smoothed her hand over the last page of one of her old high school scrapbooks. The pages, stained and brittle, some stuck together, others bent or torn still blended together to tell one cohesive story.

She felt a smile emerge, but her heart ached as she regarded a picture taken after her high school graduation. In it stood she, Justin, and a handful of their old friends all in caps and gowns, in front of the old school. She was smiling for the camera but Justin was looking at her instead, with an expression that seemed to say that her smile was all he ever needed.

He hadn't been looking at her that way today, however. Something in him, his patience or tolerance for her, had snapped. Maybe he'd never look at her that way again. The breath caught in her chest. She squeezed her eyes shut and shook her head.

No. She was being melodramatic. She'd apologize. They'd be all right within a few days.

When she opened her eyes, she had to blink to be sure that the dark silhouette of him standing in the barn door, backlit by the sun, was real and not a figment of her imagination. He strode purposefully toward her and, without a word, began gathering up the belongings strewn about her feet and putting them back into the boxes. Then he stacked the boxes where they'd been before. He gathered the furniture he'd salvaged; a small coffee table, a cedar chest, a rocking chair, and added them to the collection.

"That rocker belonged to Richard's mother." She could barely do more than whisper. "I probably should get it back to her. I haven't been in touch with his family since I left here. After the funeral, they'd call every few days to check on me, but after the storm..."

Justin stopped shifting the furniture and gave her a long, hard look.

She swallowed. "As far as they knew, I died in that tornado, and I just..." Her voice trailed off and a fresh batch of tears pooled in her eyes.

"You just ran off without a thought for anyone but yourself."

She gasped and a tear rolled down her cheek. But

her spine stiffened. All her defenses went up. She'd been twenty-six years old and had already suffered more untimely loss than many people experience in a whole lifetime. God had abandoned her, or at least it felt like He had. She'd had a right to be angry and bitter, she'd had a right to go her own way after years of doing it God's way and then losing everything. *Everything!* Her parents, her husband, her home.

But indeed, O man, who are you to reply against God?

The verse rolled through her mind gently at first, like a tidal wave at its birth. But it gathered strength quickly, dislodging and toppling those defenses, one by one, until it was painfully clear that there was no disputing what he said. Running away with no thought for anyone except herself was exactly what she'd done. And there was no acceptable excuse for it. She looked down at the small opal ring he'd saved for her.

Justin made a final adjustment to the placement of the furniture, then he pulled the tarp back over one side of the heap. "All this stuff'll be OK here until you can arrange to move it."

She nearly gasped again. She hadn't even known these things still existed until this afternoon. Now he expected her to make arrangements to move them. Like they meant nothing to him. Like they had been in his way all these years. He crossed to the other side of the stack and pulled the tarp the rest of the way up and over it. Then he turned and strode to the door.

Elaine hustled to catch up. She stopped him with a hand on his arm as he paused to turn off the light. "Justin, please wait."

He turned around to face her. The look on his face said *talk fast.*

"At least let me apologize."

He folded his arms across his chest. "Go ahead, then."

She took a deep breath, but didn't know what to say now that she had her chance. *I'm sorry* seemed a tad understated given how angry he was. But she didn't know that she'd done anything wrong enough to have to get down on her knees and beg his forgiveness.

"Tell me, what are you sorry about, Elaine?"

She pressed her cool fingertips to her hot, inflamed eyes and took a deep breath, willing the right words to come out when she started to speak. "I'm sorry." She placed both her hands on his folded arms. "I...It wasn't even a date, really. Aunt Laura invited Boyd over. Not me." It sounded lame, a meager defense.

In hindsight she could see that she should have followed him to his truck and insisted that he stay. But it was too late for such measures now, and she didn't have a clue what else to say anyway. "I'm sorry if it hurt your feelings, Justin. I didn't mean to."

He softened slightly with a weary sigh, but his anger still simmered close to the surface. "No. I know." He shook his head. "It's my own fault that it bothers me to know that your only attachment to me is because I can fix your back porch or kitchen floor."

"That's not true," she said softly. There had to be sufficient words to tell him exactly how much remorse she felt, not just for what happened this week, but for everything, her whole history of relating to him.

"Maybe it really *is* my fault." He reached up with one hand and pinched the bridge of his nose, squeezing his eyes shut for an instant before opening them to look at her again. "Maybe I've just totally misread everything that's happened between us since you've been home."

She reached out for him again. "No, Justin—" But the moment she touched him he evaded her.

"I thought we were making some kind of connection." He uttered a short bitter laugh. "Can't believe I was stupid enough to believe you finally had feelings for me. Real feelings."

"But Justin, I do!" *God, what do I do now? What do I say?*

She *had* real feelings for him, but those feelings confused her completely. Desperation clamped like a vise around her heart, which continued to beat, faster than ever. She could see exactly where this confrontation was headed, but she couldn't let it go there.

He wanted something from her; an understanding, a commitment. But she couldn't do that yet. Neither could she let him give up on her coming to love him, because she wanted to. She just couldn't.

Richard...

"Since you've been back it feels like everything I do is all for you." His voice was taut with intensity. "And you keep acting like there's a real reason for me to believe...You look at me, and smile at me, and touch me as if...as if you feel something for me. And now there's Boyd Wendall having dinner at your house, and taking you out for coffee—"

"Why have you never *told* me this? Never, Justin. Not way back in school. Not before I got married, or after Richard died. Not since I've been home."

"How can you stand here and act like you never realized it?" He glowered at her for a very long moment, taking deep breaths, deliberately steady.

She couldn't meet his penetrating stare because he was right.

"Let me tell you now, Elaine." His voice was hoarse, and tears lurked in his eyes, though none fell. "When I was nine years old, on the last day of school we were all walking to the bus stop and you smiled at me. There wasn't anything special or unusual about it. But it was like, all of a sudden, I saw you for the very first time. I've loved you since then. I didn't tell you back in school because I was a stupid kid. I didn't tell you before you got married because you weren't here. And when you moved back here with your husband there wasn't much point, was there? And after he died..." He took in a sharp breath, almost like someone had dealt him a physical blow. "He was my friend, too, Elaine. What kind of man would I have been if I'd said anything about it then? How would you have taken it then?

"Now, I wake up in the morning, get out of bed and face the day because I *might* see you. *You* are what I think about. You're what I dream about. But, in case you didn't get the point, let me just come right out and say it. *I love you*, Elaine. All this time I've loved you."

A sob erupted from the deepest part of her heart, and she reached up to cradle his face in her hands.

Richard...

"Do you love me?"

It felt like her heart stopped.

Richard...

She loved Richard. She missed Richard, her husband. Her mind swirled with a thousand little memories of him. She couldn't let him go. Their time together had been so short and his death so sudden and unexpected, and she wasn't yet prepared to let him go.

But Justin still stood in front of her, his question burning up the space between them.

"You know I love you." A tear fell.

His mouth set into a grim line "I know *how* you love me." He reached up and took her hands in his and lowered them from his face. "And it's not enough."

"Oh, Justin. Please don't—"

He shook his head and let her go. "I can't be that kind of friend to you anymore."

"You don't mean it." She reached out for him again. He didn't rebuff her, but nor did he respond. "You're angry with me, and rightfully so. You feel like I've been stringing you along, but that's not how it is. I just...I just can't..." She let her voice trail off.

"You just can't with me, you mean." He shook his head and turned away, slow steady strides carrying him outside the barn. She followed, unable to formulate another coherent argument as her mind reeled. This was unthinkable. She pressed a hand to her forehead. She had to have misunderstood him.

He unbolted the barn door and swung it closed. "Just let my mother or me know when you'll be coming for your things."

"Justin, I'm—"

"Just go, Elaine." He slid the bolt back into place, and stood facing the barn, waiting for her to leave.

She pressed a hand over her mouth to stop the swell of sobs that threatened. She knew exactly what he needed her to say, but she couldn't. As much as she wanted to she couldn't bring herself to betray Richard in that way. Even if she could, the words would come too late now.

A glance at the ring which still encircled her left

ring finger brought another stab of grief. Richard was gone. But in her heart she was still married. She couldn't give her heart to Justin, not completely. That's what he wanted and deserved.

She turned and took a few slow steps, almost positive that he'd have a change of heart and call her back to him. But he didn't. So the pace of her steps increased steadily until she had covered the distance of the pasture back to the house and her car. A sob broke free as she pulled open her car door and crawled inside. Then another as she pulled the door closed. She folded her arms across the steering wheel, pressed her forehead to them, and wept. She'd always tried so hard to keep her emotions in check. Loss after loss had plagued her, and she'd always been able to keep her pain bridled, letting it out in small increments, trying to relieve the pressure without losing control of its power. But now something inside had finally broken.

ॐॐ

Justin pulled his keys out of the ignition and stared at them for a moment. *Lord, did I do the right thing?* It sure seemed right at the time. The thought of her upset and hurting at all brought an anguish to his heart that he almost couldn't take. But the thought that tonight he'd been the cause of it...

He took a deep breath, opened his truck door, and slid out, turning back to reach across the seat for a small box of his things. Her car was parked in its usual spot in the driveway. At least she'd come straight home, she hadn't run off or gone and done something crazy.

The chilly night air nipped at his face and fingers

as he trudged up the garage stairs to his new place. But the difference between the physical chill in the air and the one around his heart was barely distinguishable. He unlocked the door, pushed it open, and stepped inside. Snug warmth enveloped him, the likes of which he hadn't felt all winter except in someone else's home. That old mobile home had probably never been warm like this, even decades ago when it had been new. But the heater in this place worked. He'd sleep here tonight.

He carried his box into the bedroom, set it on the bed, and turned to feel around on the wall for the light switch. *There.* He switched it on and turned back for the bed, but stopped, brought up short by the sight of it.

Last time he'd been in this room it had been stripped down to the mattress. But now a green bedspread covered it, turned back to reveal crisp, clean, white sheets and soft pillows. An ache rose up in the back of his throat. *Elaine.*

He heaved a sigh and reached up to rub the back of his neck. He'd been too hard on her this afternoon. She did care for him. She did think about him, at least she had before she saw him this afternoon, enough to make up a bed for him so he wouldn't have to at the end of a long day.

He should apologize.

*God...*What had he done? What had he been thinking, telling her he couldn't be her friend anymore? It sounded idiotic now that he thought about it. He squeezed his eyes shut and shook his head. Then he'd told her to leave.

This is not what he wanted. He bolted from the bedroom and went for the door. Clearly she regretted her actions. She'd tried to tell him so, but he'd lashed out recklessly in his anger. Now he wished he could take it all back. He paused on the garage steps and glanced toward her room. The light was on and he could see her through the open blinds. Her back was to the window, but she stood with her face buried in her hands. She looked up and started moving, pacing, back and forth.

Wait.

The prompting came quietly and he pushed it aside, jogging the rest of the way down the steps.

Give her time.

He shook his head. No. To give her time would only make things worse. He had to make this right. Now.

He crossed the yard in fewer than ten strides and bounded up the back porch steps. He pounded on the door. "Miss Laura?"

"Come in, Justin."

He pushed the door open and stepped inside. Laura was seated at the kitchen table, a full cup of coffee in front of her.

The furor coming from upstairs commanded his attention and he glanced in the direction of the noise. Her strides were heavy, back and forth on the wood floor. She must still have her shoes on. Something slammed. Some piece of furniture scraped or scooted on the floor. Then silence descended.

"What's she doing up there?"

Laura rested an elbow on the table, touched her fingers to her forehead, rubbed it a few times, then settled her chin into her palm with a sigh. "Packing."

"She's *what*?" He took a step backwards.

"I tried to talk some sense into her. But she said

with you right out back I don't really need her to stay."
Laura's eyes brimmed. She cast him a quick glance
then looked down into her coffee.

He rubbed a hand across his eyes and dropped it
heavily to his side again. It didn't matter. A lifetime of
being used, and lately even led on by her entitled him
to be a little angry, didn't it? At the very least it entitled
him to speak his mind. "And now she's packing to
leave?" *Again.*

Laura nodded.

Justin shoved both hands through his hair and cast
another glance at the ceiling. She was running away
again. Just like last time. He took a few paces and a
deep breath. OK, what were the options here? He
could go upstairs and try to reason with her. He could
apologize. He could beg her not to go. He wanted to.
He wanted to rush up those stairs, take her in his arms,
and beg her not to go. *Again.*

But, no. Why should he? He'd tried that before
and she'd climbed right aboard that bus without so
much as a glance back. And then five years with no
word...

A little spark, perhaps leftover from his
confrontation with her earlier, caught fire in his heart
and began to smolder, then blaze. He shook his head.
There were two options here tonight.

"Aren't you going to try to stop her?" Laura raised
her misty gaze to his.

He shook his head. "Not this time."

"She won't come back."

Justin cast another glance upward as the anger and
anguish fought it out within him. "If that's all we mean
to her, then let her go."

❧❧

Elaine sat down on the edge of her bed and dropped her head into her hands, unable and finally unwilling to stop the sobs that tore through her. What had happened tonight was yet another miserable experience to add to the series that had gone before, all summing up to an irreparably crappy life.

She pushed hands through her hair, dropped them into her lap and sighed heavily. *No, not all of it.* She closed her eyes as an image of Richard pushed its way to the forefront of her memory.

He sat beside her on a cool stone bench under a shady live oak. It was early September, probably the hottest day that year. But a light breeze lifted the oppressiveness of the heat, and ruffled his dark blond hair. He smiled at her, that magnetic, dimpled smile, and time stopped for a few seconds before he pulled a small, royal-blue velvet ring box out of his pocket, and opened it.

She'd gasped as the tears surged. The proposal hadn't been unexpected. She just hadn't expected it right then. Her fingers had trembled as he slid the small diamond solitaire onto her finger. Then he had kissed her.

Elaine took a deep breath and opened her eyes, blinking away the mist of tears. The solid gold of that ring still encircled her finger. She flattened her hand to look at it.

No. Richard's proposal hadn't been what she'd envisioned, or expected. But it had been perfect. More than that, it had been good, as had all of her moments with him—even in her grief at the loss of her parents. Their life together, living in the parsonage...Good, right, all of it. She grew to love that old house. She closed her eyes again and could almost feel the warm evening breeze she'd enjoyed so many times on the front porch swing, watching the sun set.

She had felt blessed then. But not only then.

One by one the memories washed over her. Not only of her marriage to Richard, but of her life with her parents; first days of school, family vacations, holidays. She could see the smile on her mother's face as they spun around and around in a giant teacup at Six Flags. She'd been too little to fight the centrifugal force of the ride, and had ended up squished hard against her Mom as they spun. But nothing had ever been so fun.

The day her parents left her, after getting her moved into the dorm room at college, her father had gathered her to him in a long embrace. She could still remember the scent of his cologne, the warm security of his arms around her, the sense that he was holding on one last time before setting her free. He'd pressed a kiss into her hair and told her how proud he was of her.

Another tear fell. Whether she *felt* blessed now or not, she had *been* blessed. And nothing that had happened since invalidated those blessings. And even if it did somehow, what right did she have to question it?

But indeed, O man, who are you to reply against God?

She buried her face in her hands and slid off the bed onto her knees. "God, I'm sorry."

When had she decided to completely ignore the fact that, despite the heartaches she'd encountered, far more of her life had been good? When had she become so completely selfish? Like she was the only person ever to lose parents or a husband so young. Like God betrayed her. When had she decided that she *wanted* to live this way?

She couldn't remember. But she did remember standing in that empty field, not very long ago, determined to dredge up every painful memory she could recall just so she could continue to wallow all alone in the grief and bitterness that had become her tenuous shelter.

Shall we accept good from God and not adversity?

Here there were people who loved her, needed her, and by the grace of God, still wanted her around. She swiped away her tears and looked at the open suitcase on her bed.

And here she was, packing to run away again.

She sighed heavily and closed her eyes, more tears falling. "This is not what I want," she whispered. "Not anymore. God, forgive me for wasting so much time and energy trying to keep You away. Forgive me for daring to blame You. Forgive my hard heart and heal me. I want to come home."

Peace and comfort, like she hadn't felt in years, encompassed her heart and filled her soul. She *was* home, and she would heal. She rose from her knees and began pulling out the clothes she'd so haphazardly thrown into her suitcase. It was time she became a real help to Aunt Laura instead of just biding time until she could make another getaway. Elaine draped a shirt around a hanger and returned it to her closet. Aunt Laura would be thrilled with this change of heart.

But what would Justin think? She and Justin would probably never be the same again. But she didn't want things to remain the same between them. She loved him. Elaine gasped softly as realization dawned. She loved him, she wanted to be with him, and he had finally given up on her. She could run right back to him tonight and tell him what had just happened, how her heart had changed. That she loved him and wanted him. But would he believe her?

She sighed. Probably not. She'd never given him a reason to believe her.

So give him one now.

How? What could she possibly do to prove to him that she loved him the way he loved her?

Show him.

Show him, how? By pursuing him even though he might reject her? By finally considering his feelings before tending to her own?

That was it! She would do it. She would finally be there for him like he always had for her. She'd just be there. She would risk her heart and her pride for him. She would be there, waiting for him to come around, just like he'd been waiting for her all these years.

Elaine wiped away her tears and took a deep determined breath, unpacking her suitcase with a new sense of purpose. Starting tomorrow she would show him.

11

Her car was gone.

Justin took a deep breath and let it out slowly, tamping down the ache in the back of his throat as he pulled his door closed behind him. He paused on the top stair and glanced at her window. Her room was dark now, her car was gone, and so was she.

Well. All right then. He went down the stairs at a jog. No point in pretending it surprised him. A strong, chilly gust blasted him when he cleared the bottom step and the shelter of the garage. He picked up the pace toward his truck and climbed in quickly, starting the engine and letting it idle. He cast another glance up at her window. This may not be the first time she'd done this. But it hurt just as badly.

Twelve years ago, the first time she'd left here, she had gone off to college. He'd consoled himself with the certainty that after the traditional four years she'd come home, and he'd have established his own career in law enforcement. At that point, he'd be better suited to pursue her, and she'd fall in love with him, and marry him. They'd buy a house, raise kids, enjoy grandkids, and grow old together. That had been his dream.

He uttered a short, bitter laugh and rubbed his hands together, breathing warm air onto them to fend off the chill. But she hadn't come home after the customary four years. And when she finally had come back, she'd brought a husband with her.

Anger and anguish had driven her away the second time, but he'd known without a doubt that she'd return within a few weeks if not a few days. And he'd take care of her. Help her to heal. Show her that he could be everything she needed in a man. But the weeks had stretched into months, which had turned into years. Years during which his own life had gone totally wrong.

He glanced up toward her window again.

Miss Laura had said last night that Elaine wouldn't come back if she left this time. But he didn't buy it. She'd be back. And then she'd leave again. This tailspin of hers wouldn't end without her making a conscious decision to stop it.

Justin put the truck in reverse and positioned himself to drive away. He'd been right not to go to her and beg her to stay last night. He loved her. He always would. But he couldn't do this again. It hurt too much. And the worst part was that she didn't even seem to notice the power she had to break his heart. Or maybe she just didn't care.

He shook his head and heaved a burdened sigh. That wasn't true. He was her best friend, at least that's the way she saw it. She cared. Just not as much as he did. As of now his dream of a future with her was over. She was gone, for good as far as he was concerned.

❧❧

Elaine squared her shoulders and pulled open the front door of the Blithe County Sheriff's Department.

She bit down on her bottom lip as the urge to turn around and run seized her. But she stood her ground. For this new leaf she'd turned to be real, she had to make a serious effort to find a permanent job. And this was the best—the only—lead she had.

She smoothed a hand over her straight khaki skirt and strode across the waiting area. The building was completely silent except for the click of her heels on the hard floor echoing through the starkly furnished vestibule. A woman peered out at her through a window in the wall opposite the door she'd just come in, smiled, and slid a clear panel aside. Probably bullet proof. A small shudder ran through her.

"Morning. What can I do for you?"

Elaine stepped up to the window, swallowed and cleared her throat. "Hi, I'm Elaine Mallory. I was hoping to see Ed Lacey."

"About the receptionist position?"

Elaine nodded. "Yes."

"Oh, thank goodness!" The woman gave a huge, dramatic sigh. "It's getting to where we can't find anything around here. I'm Robin, the daytime dispatcher. Come on back. Ed's in his office."

Robin reached under the counter. There was a buzz and the door beside her window popped open. Elaine pushed it the rest of the way and stepped through.

"Ed said things were getting a bit disorganized." The metal door slammed shut behind her.

"Hah!" Robin cast her a good-natured glance and turned down a wide corridor. "He has a gift for understatement." Robin rounded the corner and stepped into the first door she came to. "Elaine's here."

Ed looked up from the papers on his desk, and his

face brightened. He stood up. "Elaine! Good to see you, girl. Come on in." He came around the desk and pointed her to a chair. "Thanks, Robin."

Elaine sat down and folded hands in her lap as Robin's departing footsteps faded to silence. She took a deep breath and let it out quietly as she could. It had become abundantly clear last night that what she wanted was to come home. To rebuild her life here. So why was the impulse to run, to get into her car and drive until she could go no farther, still so strong?

She took another breath and pushed her question out before the impulse got the better of her. "I was wondering if the receptionist job was still available."

"It's really more of an office manager. I have the paper work right here." Ed reached behind him to his desk and retrieved a file folder from one corner. He leaned back against his desk and studied her for a moment, his expression slightly pained and yet hopeful. "So, you've decided to stay?" His tone was heart-warmingly paternal. Something about it put her a little more at ease.

She nodded. "Yes, sir."

"Good. You can sit right in here and fill out these forms." He handed her the folder. "It may take a few days for the results of your background check to come back, but I don't think there's any reason you can't go ahead and start right away. Unless you have an arrest record somewhere that I don't know about."

She reached for the folder and glanced up at him. His tone was light but his gaze was intent, expecting an answer.

"Um, no." She grinned before she could stop herself. "No. Maybe a speeding ticket or two."

"All settled up?"

"Yes."

He studied her for a long moment. "All right, then. Let's get those filled out. Then we'll get your fingerprints. Then I'll show you around."

She nodded and flipped open the folder, then his words caught up with her. "Fingerprints?"

"For your background check."

"Oh."

"You get started on that, and I'll be back in a few minutes."

Elaine nodded as he pushed himself away from his desk and left the room. She glanced around, hardly daring to move. Just walking into this building intimidated her. How was she supposed to work here?

But she had to. She needed a job, and this was probably the best one available in the whole county. And Ed had basically handed it to her, as if he'd been waiting just for her to come along and fill it.

She settled herself with a determined breath and perused the contents of the first form, a pretty standard job application. She took a pen from Ed's desk and put it to the paper to fill in the first blank, but stopped before making a mark.

So you've decided to stay?

Ed's question reverberated through her mind. She nodded. Yes. And she needed this job if she and Aunt Laura were going to make ends meet and still have anything left over. She filled in her name, address, phone number, social security number.

Drivers license number? She'd have to look that one up. She reached for her purse.

This is permanent. No easy way out without really letting people down this time.

Permanence. Responsibility. Stability. It's what she

wanted. She yanked her wallet from her purse, opened it, fished out her driver's license.

Why bother?

The thought stopped her cold.

Justin's through with you. Aunt Laura doesn't need you. Why stay? What's the point? Do you really think you're going to change his mind?

She squeezed her eyes shut and shook her head. Where was the resolve she'd felt just last night? Her hand shook a little, but she wrote her driver's license number in the appropriate space. These doubts were just the byproduct of years spent running away, of living for herself. It would take a little time to readjust to a life in which others depended on her. But it would come. She nodded. It would.

Education was next on the application, highest level completed first. Bachelor of Arts. Field of study: public relations. She gave an amused little grunt. That might actually make her sort of qualified for this job. Institution: Southern Methodist University.

He doesn't want you anymore!

She took a deep breath and clutched the pen more tightly. She decided to stay because she was tired of being alone and she didn't want to live that way anymore. She could be a help to Aunt Laura. And, regardless of whether Justin ever forgave her, this is where she belonged.

ॐॐ

"No ink?" Elaine tried to steady her hand as Dale Santos pressed and rolled her finger over some sort of scanner.

"Not anymore." He checked his computer monitor

before moving on to her next finger. "Relax, Miss Elaine. You're not under arrest."

She bit her lip and took a deep breath, choosing to focus, not on the procedure she was subjecting herself to, but rather on the fact that this deputy, only about eight years younger that she, persisted in calling her *Miss Elaine*. It made sense, though. Dale had been in the church youth when Richard had been pastor. He had always called her *Miss Elaine*. It had suited her then. "Bet you never thought you'd be fingerprinting the preacher's wife."

Dale grinned and shot a glance at Ed who stood beside her. "No, ma'am." He checked the monitor again. "Last one."

She jumped when a door beside her crashed open.

"Howdy, Sheriff! Didja miss me?" Laban Sadler, Junior, staggered into the corridor, steered by a deputy who had hold of one of his arms. His hands were cuffed behind him, and he reeked of alcohol.

"Didn't give me much chance to, did you."

It had been years since she'd seen Junior, even before she left. He wasn't a prize specimen of a man then, but he'd evidently fallen considerably since. He'd been the school bully until high school, when he had dropped out to pursue his crazy professional bull riding dreams. He'd never been any good at it. Elaine caught a glimpse of a big silver belt buckle under his half-untucked shirt. Probably it was store bought rather than won through any actual rodeo skill.

"Elaine! Is that you?" Junior staggered her way a couple of steps before the deputy redirected him to a nearby bench. "Hey, girl! When did you get back in town? What are you in for?"

She bit down on her lip to stifle an inappropriate

laugh. Was he serious? He was so drunk she couldn't tell. But either way, laughter would probably only encourage or enrage him. "Um, a job."

"What, here?" Junior swung his head to one side, trying to clear his stringy hair away from his eyes, then surveyed her figure with lewd appreciation. "Well, won't you make a pretty little deputy sheriff! Too bad your old friend Justin doesn't work here anymore. You seen him since you've been back?"

"Shut up, Junior." The deputy who brought him in gave him a nudge.

"Sure is a shame, what happened to him." There wasn't a whole lot of sympathy in his tone.

"What's the charge this morning?" Ed crossed the corridor and stepped between her and Junior.

"Disturbing the peace." The deputy replied. "Public intoxication. The usual."

Junior leaned way over until he could see around Ed's form. "Hey, Elaine." He affected a whisper, as if what he had to say was for her ears only, not noticing that everyone else in the room stopped to look at him. "I should be out of here in a day or so. Maybe we could get together. Do a little catching up. What do you say?"

"I said shut up, Junior." The deputy shoved him maybe a little harder than was necessary.

"OK, OK." Junior sat up and leaned back against the wall behind him. "I'm just bein' friendly. Tryin' to talk to an old friend. Nothin' illegal about that, is there? I have rights, you know."

"You have the right to remain silent." Dale's voice drew her attention to his face. He chuckled at his own joke. The other men followed suit, even Junior. Feminine laughter floated out of the dispatcher's office as well. "Don't mind him, Miss Elaine. He's pretty harmless. You'll get used to him."

She shook her head, seized by a memory of how Junior had once snatched from her hands a box of paper dolls she'd brought to school for show and tell. He'd torn the heads off the little dolls and scattered the tabbed clothes all over the playground, laughing as he stomped them into the dirt. She felt a shudder pass through her. "I've known Junior since kindergarten. I don't think I'll ever get used to him."

Dale gave a nod. "Well, let's try that last print again. Then we can get you out of his way."

❧

They were the kind of late winter clouds that looked like they wouldn't be clearing out anytime soon. Elaine stepped out of her car and surveyed the sky. The morning had been bright and clear but around noon she'd noticed the change through the front door of her new workplace. The cloud cover hadn't rolled in, like thunderstorms tended to do, but rather seemed to descend, like a big, heavy, wet blanket that wasn't going anywhere. She probably had just a few minutes before the rain would start.

Thankfully, the ground was dry for now, unlike the last time she'd walked up this grassy slope. The path was the same one she'd taken then. Maybe it hadn't been quite as chilly, but it had been a little later in the year. Springtime.

The grass here would be fresh and green a few weeks from now. The tree branches would be full with leaves. A layer of pink wild primrose would blanket the ground in large patches on the meadow to the east. It felt like only yesterday. The slope leveled off and she walked a few paces farther until she reached it.

Richard Eugene Mallory, the headstone read. *Beloved husband. Devoted son.*

She closed her eyes, vaguely recalling the day they chose the stone. Richard's mother had held her hand as they decided on the gray granite and the simple epitaph. If his parents hadn't been here to help, nothing about his funeral would have been arranged properly. She'd been too stunned to think straight, existing in a foggy plane of consciousness in which nothing moved at the proper speed and she expected him to call any minute telling her he was on his way home.

"Oh, Richard." Elaine buried her face in her hands and let the tears come once again. It was excruciating the way she wanted him back, the way she wanted to feel him warm and alive beside her, holding her hand, kissing her face, telling her that everything would be all right.

The thought of his body buried deep beneath the cold sod, lifeless and decomposing, was almost more than she could bear. She dropped to her knees and pushed her hair back away from her face.

"Baby, I miss you so much." She reached out and touched the cold, hard granite as if it could somehow connect her with him one more time. "I didn't even get to tell you goodbye. I didn't get to tell you I was sorry for being so irritated with you for going to town to help sandbag that morning."

It had been lunch time and she'd been expecting him home.

"Elaine?" He had come through the front door calling her name, an unusual urgency in his tone. "Baby?"

His voice came to her from the recesses of memory. She had been in the kitchen fixing chicken salad for lunch. Instead of greeting her with his usual hug and kiss, he went straight through the kitchen to the utility room. Maybe that's what had set her off. He came out carrying his waders.

"Are you going fishing?" Her response had been a little testy, but he didn't seem to notice.

"I'm going into town to help sandbag."

"What?"

"They say the creek has turned into a river, and it's rising fast. Hal McCoy called and asked if I could help get some men together to step up his sandbagging progress."

Hal McCoy was the epitome of a high maintenance church deacon. It seemed there was always some personal crisis of his that required Richard's immediate attention. And those crises always seemed to occur when Richard was supposed to be at home with her. More and more lately this church had been demanding his personal time. And not just time. Now Hal actually wanted Richard to go to town in the torrential rain and put his own safety in jeopardy to save a convenience store that he'd foolishly built so close to the creek, which flooded every few years. The look on her face must have given her unkind thoughts away because a knowing grin slid across her husband's face.

"His store could flood. It probably will anyway."

"Then what's the point in you going down there in the pouring rain, sloshing around in dirty water and getting sick?"

"He would do the same for us." He kissed her on the cheek then, but her response had been cold. "I'll see you later on."

Elaine sniffed and wiped tears from her cheeks, then dropped her hands into her lap. She had been sorry for her attitude as soon as she heard the front door close behind him. She had fully intended to greet him at the door when he got home with a warmer kiss and an apology. She never got the chance.

"I'm sorry." She whispered now instead.

Did this make her crazy? Sitting here on Richard's grave, talking to his headstone as if he could hear her? Hopefully he couldn't see her from where he was now.

"Oh, you'd be so ashamed of me if you could." She closed her eyes and dropped her head. "These last five years have been so hard. And I...I've been at my absolute worst. I've been selfish and thoughtless, and so bitter. I've been angry with God for taking you." She blinked and another tear fell. "And I know you're home now. You're in the best possible place, and I've been so angry with Him for taking you there. What kind of person does that make me?"

Richard would never have wanted her to live this way. He was always so full of life, so content with whatever happened.

"But I'm going to be better now. I'm going to quit running away from God. I'm going to stay here and help Aunt Laura. I got a job today, at the Sheriff's Department." She sniffed and grinned. "Can't you just see me working behind the bullet-proof window?"

She felt her grin fade. "Justin doesn't work there anymore."

Elaine bit her lip and glanced down at her hands as another swell of tears rose. "I've fallen in love with him." The words were barely more than a whisper. She cleared her throat. "I'm sorry, baby. I still love you, and

I miss you so much. But I love him, too. I don't know how that's possible."

Not that it really mattered given the confrontation she and Justin had only yesterday and what he had said about not being able to be her friend anymore.

Don't give up.

The thought came on a cool gust, as if Richard himself had whispered it into her ear. She breathed deeply and raised her face to the swirling dampness of the mist forming around her.

Remember the decision you made last night. Be there for him and don't give up. Persevere.

Persevere.

Elaine nodded and pushed off the ground as the mist began to swirl. For a moment she hesitated, rooted to the spot by an oddly comforting ache, reluctant to leave so soon after having taken so long to come to this point. Still feeling like her soul had somehow, briefly, reached out and touched Richard's. But the mist turned to drizzle and she hurried back toward her car. She climbed in and got the door closed just as the drizzle turned to a soft shower.

12

Justin stepped out of his truck, pocketed his keys, and ran a hand across his chin, staring at the house as if the force of his will alone could allow him a peek inside to see just what exactly was going on with Elaine. For a whole week he'd stayed clear of the house. A whole week, waking up in the morning to find her car gone, and coming home in the evening to find it right back in its usual place.

Every evening he'd resisted the impulse to march up the back porch stairs, pound on the door and demand to know why she hadn't run off, and what took her away from the house before him every morning—even though logic told him it was a job. *She'd taken a job.* And that meant she intended to stay. Didn't it? But for how long?

He shook his head and turned for the stairs that would lead him home. It didn't matter. He'd only make himself crazy by dwelling on it. Time to let her go. And he did, just like he had every night this week.

Thankfully the impulse to go over and demand answers grew weaker by the day, the trip up the stairs to spend the evening alone in his apartment got a little easier, too. One day, hopefully soon, he'd come down for work and forget to notice whether her car was gone or not. One evening soon he'd get out of his pick up and head on up the stairs without even wondering what occupied her in there and why she hadn't run off yet. He turned back just as he reached the bottom step.

There she stood on the back porch, hand curved around one of the posts. The breeze caught the hem of her skirt and stirred it around her legs. An ache rose to the back of his throat when she gave him an unsure smile.

"You hungry?"

He shook his head, but his stomach growled.

Her smile faded and she nodded. "Well, if you change your mind, there's plenty. There always is." She turned to go back inside.

"Why didn't you leave?" His voice sounded thick, emotional, almost desperate, despite his effort to detach himself from her.

She stopped at his question, then slowly turned back toward him. Her arm wrapped around the porch post. She chewed on her bottom lip for a long moment. "I tried to." Her voice came clear and steady across the yard. "I almost did. But I wanted to stay more than I wanted to go. I'm tired of running away."

He nodded. But the war within that he thought he'd put an end to began to wage itself all over again. Elaine was here, intending to stay—at least as far as he could tell. And he still loved her so much that he could hardly keep the distance of the yard between them. He wanted to feel her arms around him, to hear her say she loved him. He wanted to cross the distance between them and do whatever it took to make her say it.

"Are you sure you won't come in for supper?" The yearning in her voice wrapped itself around his heart and began to squeeze. Her lips curved into an enticing smile. "We're having breakfast. Pancakes, bacon, eggs, biscuits, gravy..."

A faint grin tugged at his mouth. Breakfast for supper was a Maitland family tradition. He'd been a regular participant through the years. Warm light spilled from the kitchen windows into the dusky evening, appealing to him to come and share in the tradition again. He leaned forward, pulled by some force momentarily beyond his control, but righted himself quickly. Things were different between them now.

His grin faded. "No thanks."

He turned, sent a parting wave over his shoulder, and trotted up the stairs, not looking back as he slid the key into the lock and let himself inside. He tossed the keys on the end table closest to the door, and turned on the kitchen light.

Another pang of hunger assaulted him as he headed for the freezer, pulling out a frozen dinner before the thought of the meal Elaine was fixing across the yard could lure him over there and into another futile effort to connect with her.

He expelled a breath and rolled his eyes upward. Who was he kidding? He tossed the box back into the freezer and pushed the door shut. It *might* drive him crazy to dwell on all the implications of her presence here. But it was *sure* to if he sat here, alone and wondering, when he'd been invited inside and only had to ask to have all his questions answered.

Satisfying his appetite for information struck him as far preferable to staying here, nagged by curiosity, and craving pancakes.

Justin covered the distance between his place and hers at a jog. He took a deep breath and knocked on the door. When she pulled it open, the expression of pleasure on her face took his breath away.

Elaine didn't say a word, she just swung the door open and stepped out of the way so he could come inside.

"Justin!" Laura stopped tending the scrambled eggs on the stove long enough to greet him. "I'm so glad you could join us. Come in and sit down."

Justin glanced from Laura to Elaine, who crossed the kitchen, lifted a pancake off the griddle and placed it on top of a stack. "Can I help with something?"

"You could set the table, if you like." Laura's suggestion drifted across the room. "Elaine, honey, show him where the dishes are."

"Here." Elaine reached up and opened the cabinet next to her, then she reached down and pulled out the drawer where they kept their flatware. But she didn't look at him.

"Elaine's been working this week, Justin." Laura scraped her skillet full of eggs into a bowl, then looked up at him. "She's working at the Sheriff's Department."

He shot a glance back to Elaine. She made brief eye contact with him, then focused her attention once again on the pancakes. He took three plates from the cabinet set them on the counter and reached for the forks. "How's that going?"

She lifted one shoulder and tilted her head. "So far, so good."

It gave him an odd measure of satisfaction to know that she'd taken the job he'd helped get for her. He carried the plates and flatware to the table. "Have you met any hardened criminals yet? Aside from me, of course."

She laughed in a quick little burst. "No. Just Junior Sadler."

Justin paused for a second in mid-movement as he lowered a plate. His spine stiffened like always when he thought of Junior. But he shook it off and continued setting the table.

"They fingerprinted me, though."

He put the last plate in its place and looked up to find her grinning at him. She waggled her eyebrows and turned to flip a pancake.

Something about her was different. Justin crossed back to the cabinet to get the cups. She seemed lighter tonight. Less burdened, less angst filled. *Peaceful.* That's what it was. She seemed to be at peace, and not just for the moment.

Laura made her way gingerly across the kitchen and placed the bowl of eggs on the table. "Y'all continue on. I think I need to go and sit in a comfortable chair for awhile."

"You all right, Aunt Laura?" Elaine put another pancake on the stack and unplugged the griddle.

"Do you need a hand?" Justin reached for her arm.

"Oh, I'm fine, dear." Laura patted his hand and gave him a wink. "Just a little achy here and there."

"Should we get the TV trays and eat in the living room?" Elaine brought the plate of pancakes to the table.

"No." Laura spoke with an exaggerated patience that almost made him laugh. "I want to be alone."

"Why don't I get a TV tray for you, and Elaine can fix you a plate?" Justin volunteered, knowing that Miss Laura intended to clear out so he and Elaine could talk privately.

"That sounds just about perfect." Laura reached for her cane and hobbled down the hall toward the living room.

❧❧

"So you took the job at the Sheriff's Department." Justin sounded satisfied by that.

Elaine studied him covertly as he sat down at the table. When she'd opened the door a few moments ago to find him standing there, she hadn't even been able to speak. He hadn't meant it when he told her he couldn't be a friend to her anymore. He wouldn't be here now if he had. And he wouldn't keep looking at her as if he wanted to know something.

"And they fingerprinted you."

A grin slid across her face and she nodded. "Dale Santos did it. He kept calling me Miss Elaine. I felt so old."

Justin broke open two biscuits and ladled gravy over them, taking on the reflective quality of memory. "Dale's a good kid."

Elaine speared two pancakes with her fork and lifted them to her plate. "And what about you? How's your week been?"

He swallowed a bite of his biscuit, then shrugged. "It's been all right, I guess. Been working on a new house. A retired couple from Austin, building their dream house."

"What, *here*?"

The joke worked. He smiled and took another bite.

Elaine poured syrup over her pancakes and picked up her fork, but couldn't raise a bite to her mouth. His expression was relaxed, yet a tension seemed to surround him. He was definitely here for a reason; he just hadn't gotten to it. Yet.

"So, what changed your mind?" He glanced up and held her gaze. "About leaving. What made you decide to stay?"

She lowered her fork and quietly set it on her plate. "I didn't *want* to leave, Justin." She took a deep breath and let it out on a long sigh. "Last time I wanted to. This time I didn't. It's just that...I didn't know what else to do, so I..." She ended with a shrug. "I didn't know where to go. This is my home, now. It always was. I should never have run off in the first place."

He thought about that for a moment, then nodded and took another bite. Whether he believed her or not wasn't clear.

"Did it have anything to do with Boyd Wendall?"

"What?" The question astonished her. She hadn't given Boyd a single thought this week. Of course, he'd wonder about that. She shook her head. "No. It had nothing at all to do with him. I won't be seeing him again."

"Don't stop seeing him on my account."

Elaine pushed bangs out of her eyes. The statement hadn't sounded bitter or angry at all, just the opposite. Justin's tone had been casual, conversational. But behind the carefree demeanor of it, she could tell the wound was still pretty raw.

"So, what else have you been up to this week?" His tone was still casual. Not cold, but defensive.

She took a sip of water and swallowed. "I've been out to Richard's grave a few times."

Justin stopped chewing. Finally he swallowed, but didn't say a word.

Something in his demeanor, or maybe it was the statement she'd just made, brought an image of him standing on her front porch, hat in his hands, trying to break the news of her husband's death. Tears stung her eyes, but the usual anguish which accompanied that image didn't come. There was just a calm sadness, a peaceful ache. And a piercing need to know details she'd never wanted until now.

"Justin?"

He put his fork down and wiped his mouth, then raised his gaze, his pained expression saying he had a pretty good idea what was coming next.

"What was Richard doing when he died?" She cleared the thickness from her throat. "I mean, I know he was helping with the sandbags, and was swept away in the creek and drowned..." She swallowed and squeezed her eyes shut for a second to banish the image. "But why was he in the creek to begin with? What was he doing there?"

Justin took a deep breath and let it out slowly. "Um..." He leaned forward, pushing his plate away and resting both arms on the table. "He was helping to sandbag that little convenience store on the way out of town on highway eighty-four, the one right off the bridge."

He glanced at her, looking for confirmation. She nodded.

"The bridge was closed. The water was well above it, and the current was strong, but a car tried to go around the barricades and cross anyway, and it stalled."

"Whose car?"

"Um...I..." Justin shook his head. "I don't know...They were from out of town. A woman and her kid. Trying to get home.

"I got the call first and went out to see what was going on, but before we could even come up with a plan the current started taking the car with it. So we waded in to try to get them out."

Justin's mouth set into a grim line and tears welled in his eyes. He swallowed. "I made it to the car and pulled out the kid. Richard and I passed each other on the way back." His voice was thick and growing hoarse. He shook his head. "It was only a few yards, Elaine. Twenty feet at the most, that's all. Maybe that's why I didn't think it would be a problem. But the current was so strong. I was afraid *I* wasn't going to make it back."

Elaine wiped away a tear that trailed down her cheek.

"I heard him..." Justin sucked in a breath. "I heard him call for help. He must have lost his footing. He couldn't have been more than ten feet from me, but I had this kid in my arms. I couldn't...I just couldn't get to him in time."

She pressed a hand to her mouth. He looked up at her, his eyes red and brimming, his expression suddenly as haggard as if he'd just come away from the scene.

"I'm so sorry, Elaine." His voice broke, and he raised one hand in appeal.

She wrapped her own hand around it. "Oh, no, Justin. No."

"By the time I got the kid back on dry ground, Richard was gone. The water just...swept him away over the bridge and into the creek." His fingers intertwined with hers. "The hardest thing I've ever had to do was go out to your house that day and tell you..." His voice choked up and he paused for a long moment. "Especially because it was my fault."

She gasped. "Oh, Justin. Don't say—"

"He would never have gone in if I hadn't gone first. He thought we should wait for more help." He paused and closed his eyes. "We should have. But I was young and stupid and trying to be a hero."

The warmth of his thumb as it made smooth strokes back and forth against the skin of her hand soothed her a little. But her heart ached more than ever. Not only for her own loss, but that Justin blamed himself all this time.

"So many times I've wished it had been me instead," he whispered.

A quick, convulsive sob shattered what was left of her composure. "Oh, Justin. No." She let go of his hand and rested her palm against his cheek.

"When I saw the look on your face that day, and how losing him tore you up, I thought it would have been so much easier if it had just been me—"

"Please, don't say that. Please don't *think* that." She raised her trembling hand from his cheek to smooth a lock of hair back from his eyes. "I never knew. All these years you've been feeling that way, and I never knew it. I've been so selfish, and bitter, and I had no idea..."

He took both her hands in his. "I wish I could bring him back to you."

Even if she could have doubted that, even if she might have taken it as a platitude to a grieving widow, the look in his eyes left no doubt that it was the sincerest of truths. "Oh, Justin." She wrapped her arms around him and held on tight. A series of silent sobs shook him as his arms encompassed her.

"Please forgive me, Elaine." He whispered the request into her ear.

She shook her head and squeezed her eyes shut, sending a cascade of tears down her cheeks. "Please forgive *me*."

His arms tightened around her. Something was changing between them. Their relationship began to shift. They always had this tragedy in common. But until now she'd never known how fully it had impacted him. She had someone to share in her grief the whole time, and she'd never known it. Justin could have used comforting as only one who feels the same loss can give, and she hadn't been around to give it. She had failed Richard on so many levels. If he'd seen her these past few years he wouldn't have recognized her.

Slowly, the cadence of Justin's breathing began to grow more even, in time with hers. But she held on to him, like she should have done in the weeks following Richard's funeral. She squeezed her eyes shut again. When would it stop hurting? It happened ages ago but felt like only yesterday.

But talking about it, reliving it, bonded them in a new way. She had a whole new perspective on the decency of this man. Elaine sniffed and finally pulled herself out of his embrace when she felt his arms slacken about her. They both reached for their paper napkins at the same time.

"So," his voice was hoarse and a little muffled by the napkin. "You've been out to his grave this week?"

She blew her nose. "Yes."

"How was it?"

"Good." A sudden, odd sense of shyness came over her. She looked down. "Cathartic. Have you been since the funeral?"

Justin nodded. "I went out there the day they put the headstone in."

Another thing he took care of in her absence. She reached out and gave his hand a grateful squeeze.

"I never knew his middle name was Eugene." Justin grinned a little.

"He hated his middle name." A slow smile emerged through her leftover sorrow. "He'd be so mad if he knew we used it on his headstone."

"I wish I'd known that when he was alive."

"I would have told you, but he swore me to secrecy."

Justin wiped a single tear from the corner of his eye and chuckled. "I guess it's lucky for him *you* could be trusted. 'Cause that's not a secret *I* could've kept."

13

Elaine stood up straight, stretched, and wiped dusty hands on the front of her old bib overalls. This was taking longer than she'd anticipated.

Vic had backed his truck into the barn and helped her load the furniture pieces into the bed. He'd tucked them in close to the cab, like puzzle pieces, leaving plenty of room for the boxes. But she wanted to sort through a few things first, so she'd know what needed to go into the house, and what could go into storage in Aunt Laura's garage.

She glanced at her watch. She'd told him to give her an hour to repack the boxes accordingly. But here she was, an hour later. The sun was setting and she had only completed about half of her task. Irritated disappointment swelled. It would probably take her another hour just to finish the sorting, then there'd be the loading, driving back to town, and unloading. Now she'd either have to trouble Vic well after dark to finish, or on another day.

She let out a long disheartened sigh. Either way, she'd need more light. She toed a box out of her way and started around the truck. Where was that switch?

The jingle of keys on the other side of the truck told her Vic had kept an eye on the clock and had returned at the agreed time. The sound came around the truck.

"I was just looking for the light switch." She squinted against the failing light and reached out to touch the wall, finding a mass of sticky spider web, but no switch.

"It's on the other side."

Elaine jumped and turned. It wasn't Vic's voice responding, but Justin's. Her heart picked up its pace.

"Sorry, didn't mean to startle you."

"Um..." she gave her hand a shake, but the clingy threads that wrapped around it a second ago didn't budge. "I was expecting Vic."

Justin watched her, his expression unreadable.

"Spider web." She glanced down at her dusty, faded denim, and shoved hands into her pockets, resisting the impulse to reach up and make sure her hair didn't feel too totally wrecked. "Um, I've asked Vic to help me move all this stuff."

Justin nodded. "Your aunt told me you were out here."

Dusky light filtered through the rain clouds outside and flowed in through the open barn door, gently lighting the contours of his face. The faintest stubble had emerged across his jaw. Elaine balled her pocketed hands into fists to quell the impulse to reach out and run a finger along it.

"You could have asked me." He glanced over her shoulder before returning his gaze to her face. "To help you move all this."

Elaine nodded. "I didn't want to trouble you."

"It wouldn't have been any trouble." His tone was kind, maybe even a little remorseful.

"I just didn't want you to think that...To feel like I was..." she didn't feel as if she could ask for his help. She gave a shrug. "I can manage. I just figured the move would go faster with a truck. Instead of making twenty trips back and forth using just the trunk of my car..." she let her voice trail off. He wasn't interested in her reasoning.

"Well, let me help you now." Justin turned and took stock of the piles of boxes. "Are these ready to go?"

"Um, yeah." Elaine pulled a black marker out of her bib pocket. "Just let me label this one." She stooped over the last box she'd packed and scribbled its contents and destination on the side.

"Very organized." He grinned as he lifted a box, set it onto the lowered tailgate, and slid it into the bed.

Elaine lifted another and slid it in next to his. "It's been awhile since I've moved anywhere the proper way. Usually I just toss stuff into any old box and chuck it in the trunk. But I have so much more stuff all of a sudden."

Justin stooped to pick up one more.

"I know I said it before. But thank you for saving all these things. I know it took a lot of effort." Tears stung but she grinned through them, forcing them back. "I didn't realize when I walked away that day how much it would mean to still have this now."

She picked up a box and set it on the tailgate. "It was six years ago today that Richard died." She hooked her thumb around the front of her left ring finger. She had taken her wedding ring off a couple of weeks ago. Although she was growing accustomed to its absence, the void it left seemed more than physical today. Elaine raised her gaze to Justin. He had noticed the gesture. She flattened her hand against the top of the box, but he reached for it, gently stroking the bare spot with his thumb.

"I know," he said softly. "That's why I came. I wanted to make sure you were all right."

She nodded and looked down at their joined hands.

"Thank you, Justin. You've always been so good to me. Such a good friend, and I..." she let her voice trail off. A declaration of friendship wasn't what he wanted to hear. And it wasn't what she wanted to say, either. Not really.

"I don't want to be your *friend*, Elaine." He reached out and caught her other hand. "All our lives that's all we've been. I can be more than that to you."

He drew her close and surveyed the entire terrain of her face before settling his gaze once again on hers.

Her breath caught and a surge of adrenaline shot straight through her.

"I know I don't have much to offer right now. I don't make much money. My standing in the community is pretty much below average. But I'm getting back on my feet. And I love you. I can be the kind of man you need and want if you'll let me. If you're willing to be with me despite everything that's happened."

She swallowed past the rising lump in her throat. This was it. The moment she'd hoped for. *And listen to him. Standing here trying to convince her of everything she already knew.* Trying to convince *her*, when she was fully prepared to beg if necessary to convince him that he was already the man she wanted and needed. She stepped closer, until the only thing between them was their joined hands.

The rise and fall of his chest quickened. "I'll do whatever it takes to please you, Elaine, *except* just being friends. I want more than that from you." He sucked in a deep breath and let it out slowly. "I want you to love me. Not as a friend." He finally let go of her hands and slid his arms around her. "I want you to *love* me. Like I love you. Nothing less. And if you can't do that, then I'm gonna have to let go. For good. OK?"

The heat of his hands radiated straight through the denim of her overalls and the t-shirt she wore underneath. Her pulse pounded.

His penetrating blue gaze was unrelenting, questioning. *What's it going to be? Everything or nothing?*

Everything! Right here, right now. Her whole heart, the rest of her life. Everything. He was offering her another chance, and what kind of idiot would she be if she hesitated one second in taking it? How could she put into words how much she loved him, respected him, wanted him? That she could feel this way about him still shocked her so completely she couldn't express it. She opened her mouth to try. But no eloquent, tender speech came. All she could do was nod and whisper, "I can do that."

He blinked and shock registered for a second. "You can?"

Clearly, he hadn't expected that.

"OK?" His hands slid up her back, her neck to cradle her face. They were so warm that she nearly melted. Her eyelids drifted halfway shut as one of his thumbs traced her bottom lip, igniting the spark inside that had been smoldering since that evening on the garage steps.

"You love me? You're *in love* with me?" His voice was deep and thick, and charged with astonishment. She felt it vibrating within him.

"I love you," she whispered.

His touch on her firmed and he tilted her head

until she really had no choice but to look him in the eye. "Say it again."

"I love you, Justin."

Finally, after a long moment, a slow smile emerged. Yet he held on, still taking in every curve and line of her face, as if he couldn't believe what he'd just heard. Just looking at her, just hearing her say she loved him.

She was about to spontaneously combust.

"Could you please kiss me now?" Her voice was rough and barely audible.

His smile took on a whole different aspect. "I'm sorry. I didn't quite catch that."

She blinked a few times. Was he teasing her? Now? At a time like this? Finally she smiled. Of course he was. And he deserved to hear that one again, too. "I love you. Please kiss me, Justin."

His callused hands blazed a trail across her skin as they slid down to her neck. He pressed a soft, warm, moist kiss to her cheek, raising gooseflesh clear down to her toes. "Is that what you had in mind?" The question was little more than a breath in her ear.

Who was this man? And how could she have known him for so many years and not know that, in addition to everything else he'd been to her, he was capable of making her senses reel and her head swim like this. And that little breathy kiss on her cheek, while totally delightful, was nowhere near what she had in mind.

"Not exactly." A shiver passed through her.

His brow wrinkled in mock concern. "No?"

She took a deep, steadying breath. Instead of restoring a measure of control, it only served to further fill her senses. She caught the faint scent of his cologne, and something else. Her eyes drifted closed. Sawdust and wood smoke. His breath was warm against her skin, and the barn around her began to tilt and sway.

Then his lips touched hers. So soft she barely felt it. Yet it engulfed her completely. Intoxicating, but far from satisfying.

"Is that more like it?" His breaths came more unevenly now. He wasn't quite the picture of control, but he was irresistible.

Elaine nodded. "Better." The muscles under her hands tensed and twitched as she slid them up his chest, over his shoulders and his neck, finally weaving her fingers into his thick, dark hair.

Justin closed his eyes. When he opened them again all traces of flirtation were gone. He wrapped his arms around her waist and pulled her close. No more teasing, no more thinking about it.

She gently pressed her lips to his. His response was immediately intense, like an electrical arc, finishing the connection she'd started, deepening and strengthening the contact she'd made. She felt rather than heard a gasp escape as his arms closed tighter. The satisfaction of years of unrequited love on his part was tangible, building in momentum and quickly sweeping her away with it.

His arms felt so strong. Something inside yearned to get as close as she could to him. Tonight, here, now. Before something happened to spoil it.

He covered her mouth with his again and she yielded completely, even as something inside told her that her reaction to him was too much, too soon. Somewhere in the far reaches of her brain she heard the thunder outside begin to roll. But here in his arms, being loved by him, it didn't faze her. The thunder gave way to the tinny sound of raindrops on the metal roof above.

With a deep, ragged breath Justin pulled his mouth from hers. Elaine wrapped her arms around his neck.

"I love you." She whispered the words he'd been longing for so many years to hear.

He pressed his forehead to hers and closed his eyes. "Say it again," he whispered.

"I love you." She whispered the words again. "I love you. I love you."

"Please marry me, Elaine."

The breath caught in her chest. The impulse to step back and stare at him was almost too strong to resist. More thunder rumbled outside. *Marriage.* Yes. She nodded, but couldn't speak. She wanted to marry Justin. Tears surged and she laughed through them, nodding more emphatically as he pulled her into a close embrace.

"Yes, I'll marry you." She said the soft words in his ear as his arms tightened around her.

But a fiery little dart pierced her heart with the idea that, for them, happiness couldn't possibly come this easily.

14

She could feel his gaze on her. He stood a good twenty yards away, seemingly engrossed in conversation with his mother, Dot and Vic, but he was watching her. Elaine smiled secretly and turned to check the supply of paper cups under the counter of the little trailer booth the church youth group had set up for their Bluebonnet Days cold drink fund raiser.

Slow business so far this morning meant that supplies were still plentiful, but it was early yet, and the morning already quite warm. Sales would surely pick up as the day heated up and dragged on, but for now she took the opportunity to gaze furtively across the fairground midway at the man whose friendship had finally won her heart.

A slow smile spreading across his face told her that, despite her intended covertness, he was aware of her attention, and that the conversation playing out around him didn't engross him as completely as he wanted others to think.

Things might have turned out so differently for her if the little kiss they'd shared at fourteen had blossomed into another kind of relationship. But, no. If that had happened she might have missed out on Richard and the life they'd shared. And no matter how painful these last few years without him had been, she would never regret the path her life had taken back then.

Another warm smile stole its way across her face before she could stop it. But these past few weeks... She loved the feel of his arms around her, relished his kisses, dreamed now of the day when they'd be married and she could love him as his wife. She felt her smile widen, but she checked it carefully. No need to act like a giddy idiot.

When she looked up again Justin stood right in front of the booth.

"Whatcha thinkin' about?" As if he didn't already know.

"Ice." She turned her warm smile on him. "We could use a couple extra bags."

"Is that so?" He leaned across the counter for a kiss and she obliged.

"It's not a kissing booth, y'all." Elaine had totally forgotten they weren't alone. Ashley Chandler grinned at her from a corner of the booth.

"Be back in a bit." Justin said softly.

Elaine watched him go then turned to find Ashley grinning at her.

"Y'all are so cute."

"Cute?" Elaine stifled a laugh.

"Too cute for words," came a lazy drawl from outside. Junior Sadler stood, leaning against the hinged counter, materialized like an evil spirit, where Justin had stood just seconds ago.

Ashley's grin vanished and she turned away.

"You know he's a criminal, don't you?"

"You're one to talk, Junior."

Dale Santos told Elaine on her first day of work that she'd get used to Junior. And to some extent she had. Junior didn't make her nearly as uncomfortable when they brought him in drunk and disorderly. But he was free today, no handcuffs, no deputy making sure he minded his manners.

"A convicted felon." Junior took extra care to emphasize each syllable of the phrase. "Drugs, Elaine. Now me, I might enjoy one too many beers every now and then, but there's no crime in that. But Justin..." he paused, leaned closer and lowered his voice. "I heard he wasn't just using the stuff, he was selling it. To school kids. I heard they found a meth lab in his garage. Is that the kind of man you should be with? You, the preacher's wife? Really, Elaine," Junior continued. "I'm just looking out for you. I'd hate to see you get all involved with a serious criminal."

She tried to hold her tongue. She'd learned if she didn't respond, he usually got bored and went away. It had been that way since kindergarten. But *how dare he*! By what right did a total loser like Junior Sadler, the town drunk, cast aspersions and spread rumors about Justin? She could feel heat creeping up into her face and her hands began to tremble.

Junior leaned in closer as Ashley shrank further into a dark corner of the booth. "My offenses, on the other hand, are minor, and the love of a good woman like you could surely reform me. All I need is a reason to straighten up."

"I'm afraid there's little chance of reforming you, Junior." Elaine pushed out through gritted teeth.

"Aw, come on, Elaine." Junior drawled. "Don't you even want to give it a try? You know I've always kind of had a crush on you. Ever since that day you brought your paper dolls to show and tell."

"You mean the day you knocked the box out of my hand and stomped all my paper dolls into the dirt?

Is that the day you mean?"

"You know boys only tease girls they like."

"You can't be serious!"

Junior looked a little confused by her reaction. As if he couldn't fathom how she wouldn't be tempted away from Justin by a man like him, with his stringy hair and scrawny tattooed arms, the stench of too much alcohol in the haze that followed wherever he went. As if she would look back on the paper doll incident with fond nostalgia, an act of an infatuated boy rather than a bully. Junior had *way* too much confidence.

"What would your husband have to say about your association with the likes of Justin Barnet? The preacher surely wouldn't approve."

Elaine tried to still her trembling hands. She could feel her blood pressure rising. "But *you* he'd approve of." The sarcastic remark slipped out before she could stop it.

Junior just gave her a blank stare, totally missing the point. She was sick of him. Every time they brought him in at work he made some snide comment about Justin, as if he relished the thought of Justin's hardships. Now he stood with that smug look on his face, not understanding the insult she'd just tossed at him.

When a nasal little snicker came, Elaine mentally plowed over the niggling feeling she ought to shut her mouth. Suddenly *she* relished the thought of him understanding her completely.

"How dare you criticize Justin. *You*, of all people." She seethed. "What gives you the right? Justin is a good, hardworking, capable man—

Junior sneered. "He's a construction worker. No,

Deborah Pierson Dill

not even that most of the time. More like a little old handy man coming over to fix your broken window or something."

"And what do you do, Junior?" She sneered back at him. "You can't even ride a bull for eight seconds. Can you even ride a horse? You're not even half the man Justin is, and you don't know the first thing about him."

Junior's eyes narrowed and the lines of his face hardened ferociously. "Well, that's where you're wrong, *preacher's wife*." The title he gave her dripped with contempt. "I know a whole lot more than you ever will about Justin."

All the little hairs on her arms prickled and a quiet little voice inside said that it was time to back down. Ashley tried to become invisible in the corner of the booth, her face registering shock, and fear.

Junior opened his mouth to add something, but a knock at the back door of the trailer stopped him. She turned to open it, finding Justin with a bag of ice in each hand. Elaine looked over her shoulder.

Junior was gone.

రీ∞ళ

"What else did he say?" Justin looked so grim. Just the mention of Junior's name sparked animosity that radiated.

Elaine shrugged. "Nothing really. A lot of stuff about you being a hardened criminal in comparison to him. Nothing he doesn't rant on about every time he gets brought in. Nothing new." She dipped the corndog in her mustard and, bit into it. "Why does he hate you so much?"

Justin leaned forward, elbows on the picnic table, and sighed heavily . He shook his head. "I arrested him a few times. In front of his girlfriends."

"So has Dale. And Ed. And every other officer at the sheriff's department. He doesn't seem to hold a grudge against any of them. Sometimes he actually seems to enjoy himself."

"I know he always kind of liked you." Justin gave her a slight little grin and reached across the table for her hand, pulling it to his lips for a kiss.

Elaine almost snorted in disbelief. "Ever since kindergarten and the incident with the paper dolls?"

"Maybe that's where his life of crime began. Spurned by the girl he loved. He never recovered. I do believe I heard you call him a stupid butt-head that day."

She feigned indignation. "I did not." Then she grinned. "Did I?"

Justin nodded."Yep. You said, 'Junior Sadler you're a stupid butt-head and I hate you!'"

She felt her smile widen. "What did he do?"

"He just ran off laughing his evil little laugh."

"I don't remember that." She shook her head slowly. "You know, he did say earlier that he always kind of had a crush on me. And boys only pick on girls they like."

"So that's it." Justin covered her hand he still held. "He's trying to lure you away from me."

Elaine couldn't suppress her laughter. "With all his considerable charm?"

Justin's grin widened. "Is it working?"

She rolled her eyes. "I still think he's stupid."

"Ah, but no longer a butt-head. He's improved in your estimation." Justin fell silent for a moment, studying the back of her hand as he continued to stroke it. His grin faded slowly. "He detested Richard though, and I never could figure out why. I always just thought it was because Richard was a preacher and Junior was evil. But maybe he's jealous. You and I were always good friends. Maybe that's it."

She shook her head. "No. It's more than that. Just before you got there and he disappeared he said that he knew more about you than I ever would."

Justin's hand tightened around hers and he straightened up, alarm clearly showing in his expression. Cryptic as it was, that statement had struck a chord, and not a good one.

"What do you think he meant by that?"

His gaze met hers and he took a deep breath, as if trying to slow the pace of his thoughts.

"What could he know about you that I don't, or ever will?"

He opened his mouth to say something, but closed it again, and shook his head.

"*Is* there something?" She tried hard to cover the alarm in her voice. Only once had she even remotely considered the possibility that Justin might actually be guilty of the crime he'd been convicted for.

No! She dismissed the thought before it had a chance to fully develop. She knew Justin. And he wasn't guilty. But Junior's puzzling statement, combined with Justin's slowness to answer the question alarmed her. There was more to this story.

Justin took another deep breath and shrugged. "I don't know, Elaine. It's just speculation."

"About what?"

He leaned across the table, pushing aside her paper plate and unfinished corn dog. She leaned forward, too, as her heart picked up its pace.

"Elaine, the police found the crystal meth in my house, double bagged and duct taped inside the lid of the toilet tank." He paused and pressed his lips closed for a moment, as if trying to decide what to say next. "But it wasn't mine. I didn't put it there. Why would I put it *there*, in such an obvious place, if it *was* mine?" There was a desperate note in his tone. "The police came because of an anonymous tip phoned in to the sheriff's department. They didn't just happen to be there and run across it. Someone called and told them it was there. More than once."

"So this tipster called twice?"

Justin shook his head. "Four or five times!" He checked his volume and looked around. "The first time Ed called me in and asked about it. Not specifically whether I was in possession of illegal drugs. But if I was doing OK, was I under too much stress, trying to get me to open up. I kept telling him everything was fine, but he didn't believe me.

"Finally, he just came right out and asked why someone would be calling in a tip about methamphetamine in my possession. Of course I didn't have a clue what he was talking about. And he let it go. Chalked it up to misinformation or someone with a grudge. It was an anonymous tip, so there was no way to follow up on it.

"But then there was another call, and another, and Ed said he couldn't just ignore them." Justin paused. "Since I lived in town he turned the matter over to the local police and said I should just let them do their search and be done with it." He raised one shoulder in a half shrug. "Well, I didn't have anything to hide, so I said sure." He leaned back, released her hand and folded his arms across his chest.

Elaine leaned forward.

"It wasn't even hidden very well." He shook his head at the memory. "The toilet tank is one of the first places we look. Then they arrested me. Put the handcuffs on, read me my rights, put me in the squad car right there in front of the whole neighborhood. All because I had nothing to hide and I said, sure, do a search."

"What choice did you have?"

"I guess I could have said no. They would have had to get a warrant, and an anonymous tip might not have been enough to convince a judge a search was necessary. But then I would have looked guilty. If you insist on your rights people just assume you're guilty." He squeezed his eyes shut for a second, and then leaned forward again. "I always kind of suspected Junior had something to do with it. He's always hated me, even back in school. He threatened me a few times after I arrested him."

Elaine leaned closer on a sharp intake of breath. Their heads were nearly touching. "So, you think Junior did it?" She scanned their surroundings for traces of Junior or one of his buddies. The idea resonated so clearly it raised chill bumps. Junior was capable of such hatefulness. "But how would he have gotten in without you knowing about it?"

He shrugged. "I don't know. Maybe I left a door or a window unlocked. It's just a feeling I've always had." Justin reached for her hands again and fell silent as a live band started up somewhere across the fairgrounds.

"Did you tell Ed?"

He let out a blunt, bitter laugh. "Ed follows the

evidence. As he should. Criminals lie. I know that. They all plead innocent. As far as Ed was concerned, the evidence said I was guilty."

Elaine shook her head with intensity. "But he should have known better. How could Ed work with you all those years, train you, work along side you, and not know you better than that? How could he even begin to suspect you could be guilty of such a thing?"

Justin swallowed hard, and dropped his gaze to their joined hands. Clearly Ed's judgment had hurt him.

"Oh, Justin." She reached up and rested a palm against his cheek. "I'm so sorry."

He leaned into her touch. The smile he gave held the faintest traces of fading sorrow.

"Everything's all right now."

❧❧

Elaine watched the gravel path as she walked, looking up occasionally to make sure she wasn't about to run headlong into something. The band finished a set and the audience applauded as her mind clicked furiously. Junior might have had something to do with Justin's incarceration. She never aspired to be a detective. But what she felt now had to be the "hunch" she'd heard so much about. Maybe she just wanted to lay the blame on someone. Maybe that's why she latched onto the idea. But Justin had the same feeling.

The applause faded, leaving the more distant sounds of carnival rides and games to underscore the buzz of conversations going on all around.

"Justin Barnet..."

Elaine stopped short at the sound of his name

coming to her on the warm breeze. Not far away, either.

"...thinks he's somethin'..."

Just brief snatches of dialogue rose above all the other sounds. But from where? She took a few steps and the vaguely familiar voice grew more distinct, coming from around the corner of the corn dog stand.

"...no better than the rest of us."

She knew that voice. She'd heard it more than she cared to in recent weeks. It was Junior Sadler, she was pretty sure.

"Someone needs to take him down a notch or two." The voice continued more clearly. Elaine stepped quietly closer and held her breath. "I could do it, too. I've done it before, and no one ever figured it out. I could do it again."

"Just forget about it, Junior," another voice said. "Don't push your luck."

"He's been convicted once. It wouldn't be a stretch to think he could be a repeat offender."

Elaine could hear the brazen smile in his words. But she didn't realize the footsteps she heard on the gravel path belonged to him until it was too late. Junior came around the corner and ran right into her.

"Whoa there, Elaine." His eyes narrowed and searched her face. "Better watch where you're goin'. You wouldn't want to get hurt."

"Excuse me." Elaine dropped her gaze and made a move to circumvent him, but he reached out to put both hands on her shoulders.

"Now don't run off. Stay and chat awhile." The words sounded like an old friend. But the way he took hold of her elbow and pulled her toward him was anything but friendly. "I know a nice quiet spot where we can finish the talk we started earlier."

"I have to get back to the booth." She jerked her arm out of his grasp. "Dot and Ed are expecting me."

The comment hit its mark and Junior stepped back. "Well, maybe some other time, then."

Elaine pushed past him and his friend, keeping her pace normal considering the hammering of her heart. After wondering, just moments ago, what it might take to find some evidence against him, she stumbled inadvertently into an open admission. More than that. He'd been bragging about what he'd done. Hadn't he? And then he'd threatened her. Hadn't he? And now she had the evidence Ed had never been able to find; evidence that could restore Justin to his rightful position.

She stopped at the turn in the path that would lead her to the booth, and looked back toward Junior, hoping he turned and made his way in the other direction. But there he stood, staring after her with a narrow-eyed scowl on his face.

15

"You heard him say it?"

It was more a statement than a question—a doubtful statement.

"I heard him say it." Elaine nodded emphatically, on the edge of resentment, as Ed shifted his weight and leaned back in his squeaky office chair. He steepled his index fingers and touched them to his chin. His skepticism projected fully in the attitude of his posture. "I heard him say that he'd taken Justin down a notch once and that it wouldn't be hard to do again."

"Elaine that could mean anything—"

"He said he'd done it and no one ever figured it out."

"But, Elaine—"

"He said it wouldn't be hard for people to believe Justin was a repeat offender—"

"Elaine!" Ed held up his hands as he stood to cross his office and close the door. He dragged one hand across the top of his head, then rubbed his neck. "I'll admit it sounds suspicious, but did you hear him say he deliberately planted evidence to incriminate Justin."

Her jaw dropped. "Why are you so reluctant to believe Justin is innocent?"

"Why are you so insistent that he can't possibly be guilty?"

The words stung like a slap and Elaine took an

involuntary step back. "Do you really need to ask? You of all people?" The question came out just above a hoarse whisper.

Ed heaved a heavy sigh and shook his head, pausing to sit on the edge of his desk. "No. No, I don't." Another weary sigh. "Look, Elaine, I appreciate your total faith in him. I do. But there's the small matter of the evidence."

"Which Junior all but outright said he put there himself."

"Yes, but he *all but* said it. Meaning he didn't actually say it, did he? Taking Justin down a notch or two, there's any number of ways he could have planned to do that. Unless you heard him say that he planted that evidence at Justin's or he knows who did, you don't have a confession."

"Is it so hard to believe that Junior would do something like that?"

Ed let loose a blunt sarcastic laugh and shook his head. "Not that he *would*. No. He's mean and spiteful enough to do a lot worse. That boy's a ticking bomb. No, I don't doubt that he would. I kind of doubt that he could, though. He ain't the brightest bulb in the box."

Elaine felt her ire subside at Ed's shared opinion that Junior was a sorry, hateful—not to mention stupid—specimen. That was, at least, some common ground.

"Have you talked to Justin about this?"

Elaine nodded. Of course she talked to Justin. She'd talked to him first, despite Junior's lurking presence at the fairgrounds. She noticed him at the grocery store that evening—not shopping, just lurking. And this morning when she stopped at the convenience store for gas, Junior sat in his truck in the parking lot smoking a cigarette. She felt stalked, and Junior's message was clear. But it wouldn't stop her from seeking justice if she could find it.

"And he thought you should come to me with the information?"

For all the good it's done. She nodded again and sank into a chair opposite Ed's desk. What else could she have done? Where else could she have gone? Now she had some inkling of the frustration Justin must have experienced all this time, as his profession of innocence continually fell on deaf ears.

She knew in her soul she overheard Junior bragging about framing Justin for a crime he would never have committed—knew exactly what he was talking about. And she came to the proper authorities with the information, and there was absolutely no change? Maybe she should have called it in as an anonymous tip.

"I'd like to believe it, Elaine, but—"

"But what?" Elaine nearly snapped. "You're too jaded to believe that Justin's as good a man as you used to think he was? You're too afraid or ashamed to admit making a mistake?"

"Elaine—"

"I know what I heard, Ed. And I know it was Junior who said it, and I know exactly what he meant. And you do, too." She stood and pulled her purse up onto her shoulder. "And I think you've always realized the injustice of it. When I asked Justin why you didn't fight harder for him he said that you were just doing your job. That you had to go where the evidence took you. But you know Justin. Didn't you ever think that the *evidence* wasn't necessarily the truth?"

"Of course I did, but there was never any proof."

"Well, now there is!" Elaine realized where she was and with whom she spoke. She felt a hot tear fall and cast her gaze to the floor. "I'm sorry, Ed. I..."

The weight of his hand, gentle on her shoulder, made her look up. He gave her a regretful smile and a nod. Ed wanted to believe her but he'd been convinced by the evidence. The proof. He was sorry, but he just as clearly had no intention of acting on the information she'd brought him.

"I think I'll get to work now." She turned, opened Ed's door and stepped out into the hall, right into Dale Santos. "Oh, good morning, Dale." She turned and walked briskly down the hall toward the dispatcher's office, but Dale followed right on her heels.

"Is it true?" Dale asked as she dropped her purse into the bottom desk drawer. "What you overheard Junior talking about? Justin was innocent, like he said."

Elaine nodded, swallowing the urge to snap and ask him why he thought she'd lie about it. But when she looked into his eyes, she softened. His curiosity wasn't prompted by doubt, but rather by confirmation of something he already believed. His gaze held and expression of hope.

❧

A clap of thunder woke her. It exploded right overhead and rumbled slowly to its end. Elaine sighed and rolled over on her side, pulling covers up to her chin and burrowing back into her pillow. Thoughts of her conversation with Dale drifted through her semi-conscious mind. Dale never believed Justin was guilty. He always suspected Junior had something to do with it, but had no proof to back up his hunch.

Her eyelids began to feel comfortably heavy again as her mind fixed on Justin. He had kissed her tenderly after dinner with an entreaty not to worry.

"It's over and done with." He said, taking her hands and raising them to his lips. "It doesn't matter now. Things are so right, it's like it never happened."

Elaine smiled sleepily at the memory and let her eyes drift closed. But just before they closed completely she noticed a movement at her door.

The door stood slightly ajar, just in case Aunt Laura should need her for something in the night or early morning. Her mind still regularly replayed the scene of Aunt Laura amidst the rubble of the back porch after the rotten lumber had finally given way. Sometimes in the dark her sleepy mind played tricks and the half open door seemed to move.

Someone *was* in the hall. Her eyes opened as she came fully awake. She could sense it; something that wasn't normally there taking up space. She could feel the disturbance in her environment, even though she couldn't see anything in the darkened hallway.

Then the door did begin to swing open. And she wasn't imagining it. And the someone in the hall wasn't Aunt Laura.

Elaine pushed up on her elbow. "Justin?"

A laugh greeted her. Male and unnerving. Not Justin.

Her hand shot out for the cell phone on her bedside table, but he managed to get to it first, snatching it from her hand before her sleep-dulled reflexes could close her fingers around it.

He tossed the phone away and it landed soundlessly on the chair in the corner, then he raised his finger to his mouth.

"Shhhh. You'll wake your Aunt."

Junior. Her heart began to hammer.

"Junior, is that you?" She forced a casual tone. Maybe a friendly approach would work. He always seemed amiable enough when he was at the county jail. Of course, he was usually drunk. And after their last encounter, with all the insulting things she'd said, she doubted his feelings would be friendly. "What are you doing here?"

He lowered the hand he'd just shushed her with, closed her door quietly, locked it and sat down on the edge of her bed. "We need to talk, Elaine."

"We can talk anytime, Junior." She spoke a little louder than normal. If Aunt Laura was awake maybe she'd sense something wrong or hear the commotion and call for help.

"Shhh." He said again. "I told you keep your voice down. This is a private conversation."

"Can't we talk tomorrow? When I'm up and dressed and expecting you?"

"But I like you a lot better undressed and not expecting me." The crude comment had a sinister ring to it with him sitting on the edge of her bed.

"Fine." She clipped the word, but kept her full volume. "What is it you have to say, Junior?"

His hand clamped over her mouth and he leaned right into her face.

"I'm startin' to think you're being so loud on purpose." A lock of his stringy hair brushed her cheek and he reeked of cigarettes and unwashed clothes. He watched her closely for a long moment, then his expression changed. He actually grinned at her, a creepy, malevolent grin. "Now, if I take my hand away are you gonna keep your voice down?"

She nodded and felt the pressure of his hand lessen followed by the sleazy caress of his fingers on her cheek, then her shoulder. He reached over and clicked on the bedside lamp, and she squinted against the light.

Junior assessed her slowly, obscenely. She could see knowledge dawning on him. Maybe he hadn't thought this scheme through. But he now realized the position he had her in. This would not go well for her.

Finally he spoke. "I want to talk about what you heard the other day at the fairgrounds."

She made her face as blank as she could and shook her head as if in confusion.

He gave an exaggerated sigh and looked disappointed in her. "I know you heard what I said. I also know you've told Justin. And Ed Lacey. And Dale Santos." He reached out a hand and began toying with a small decorative bow on the front of her nightgown, right at the neckline. His fingertips brushed her skin.

She slapped his hand away. "What is it you think I've said, or heard, or whatever?"

He pressed his lips into a thin line and the muscles in his jaw twitched as he began to clench his teeth. He was getting mad. He leaned closer. "You want me to say it again, Elaine? You want me to confess?"

She pressed herself as far into her bed as she could. But it was futile. There was no escaping him right now. "Confess what?"

"Cause I will, baby." He pulled the covers off of her in one swift motion. "You do a little something for me and I'll confess anything you want me to."

Elaine snatched at the blanket, but he was too quick. Clearly he was completely sober. His hands were on her calves now, working their way up to her knees in a revolting caress. She gave a swift kick to one of his arms, then another, but she couldn't shake him off. His grip just got firmer as his hands kept traveling up, now on her thighs, trying to push her nightgown up.

"Stop it, Junior!" She started to push and kick in earnest panic, working her way closer to the headboard. "Stop it or I'll scream!"

He sat back and looked at her through narrowed eyes. "I thought you might." He pulled a handgun out of his waistband.

Her heart stopped and a sudden wave of nausea had her thinking she might throw up. She breathed in and out, deep and slow. She had to think, not panic. *God, what should I do? Please, Lord, what? Should I keep talking or stop talking? Should I fight or just let him...?*

"Now, tell me what you heard. Then we'll have a little fun. Maybe I'll show you just how good I *can* ride."

"What!?"

"Oh yeah, you and me." He put the gun on the table and grabbed both her arms, pressing her down onto the mattress and pinning her there. "Little Miss High And Mighty. Now tell me what you've been tellin' everybody." He pressed his face to her neck and started to sniff, before he trailed his tongue from her shoulder up to her jaw.

No, no, no! She could not just let him do what he wanted. He would have to force her, and she would fight him every step of the way.

She brought her shoulder hard against her jaw to force him out. "Are you serious?" Terror turned to indignation in an instant. She struggled to free her arms from his grip, but he was a lot stronger. She'd always thought she'd be able to best him in a wrestling match, but now she knew she couldn't. Indignation turned back into terror.

"That's good." Junior breathed. "Fight me harder. I like that."

Lord, please! This could not be happening. She was not about to be raped by Junior Sadler. She squeezed her eyes shut. *God, what do I do? Please protect me and make this stop!*

His pressure on her arms eased a little as he threw one leg over her, straddling her. "Tell me what you heard." He hissed the words into her ear, jamming one of his knees between hers trying to force them apart.

"What difference does it make now?" She hissed back, clamping her knees together for all she was worth.

His head snapped up and he glared at her.

"You think you won't get convicted for *this*!?"

He pressed up off of her, thinking.

"Aggravated sexual assault? Rape?" She jerked her head toward the gun on the table beside her. "Those carry heavier penalties than being drunk and disorderly, I can promise you. You'll be in prison for this for so long, nothing else you've done will even matter."

He remained perfectly still for a moment. What she'd said made an impression. He hadn't thought about the ramifications. She could see his mind working furiously, weighing his options. Then he shrugged.

"Well, if I'm gonna go to prison anyway, I might as well have a good story to tell when I get there."

In the second he let go of her arms to fumble with

her nightgown, Elaine twisted and reached for the gun. She clawed for it, knocking a glass of water off the table to the wood floor where it shattered.

Junior pulled her away and the back of his hand came down hard across her face. She tasted blood and tried to blink away the starbursts of color that clouded her vision. Before she could think what to do next he hit her again, and then again.

Tears stung, as much from panic as from pain. In a daze, she twisted again and tried to crawl out from underneath him. If she could just get off the bed. He'd still have the gun, but maybe she could talk some sense into him. Everyone told her he wasn't violent, just vile.

He grabbed her by the neckline of her nightgown and hauled her back to him. The fabric in his hand gave way and began to rip.

"Stop it, Junior. Please, don't do this." She pleaded. Maybe if she begged a little, admitted her vulnerability and his power, his temper would cool and he would see reason. But the urge to fight him was too powerful to resist.

"Please don't do this." He mimicked her and struck her again. "Not so special now, are you?"

She heard his voice above her own terrified sobs.

"Always thought you were too good for me, didn't you. Well, now I'm gonna take you down a notch or two, just like I did Justin."

"Justin!" She screamed, and twisted again in another vain attempt to reach the gun, but it was too far away, now.

Junior reached over and grabbed it. "Is this what you're looking for, baby?"

She stopped struggling and fixed a stare on the gun, now struggling to catch her breath.

"There now." He laughed. "That's better. Nice and gentle. See, maybe this won't be so hard after all."

With surprising competence he pulled the hammer back and pressed the muzzle to the exposed skin of her chest. The cold steel sent a shock through her.

"Oh, God, please no!" She turned her head toward the door. "Justin!" She screamed again. If he pulled the trigger, even accidentally, she'd die, but her chances of surviving this night were getting smaller by the second, anyway. If she did die, she'd do it screaming for help. "Justin!"

"Shut up!" Junior yelled, as footsteps came fast and heavy up the stairs and down the hall towards her room. He clamped a hand around her throat and began to squeeze.

The already dim light in the room grew dimmer and her head felt like it was swelling. Faintly, as if from some distance, she heard the door bust open, then a gunshot.

Then darkness.

16

A clap of thunder woke him. But it was something more, too. Like a voice in his head saying, *"Get up!"* with a sense of dangerous urgency. He swung his legs out of bed and sat up, listening for a disturbance other than the weather outside. The thunder's rumbling gradually softened then subsided as the cold spring rain began pelting his window in rhythm with the gusting wind.

Something wasn't right.

He reached for the pair of jeans he'd tossed on the foot of the bed and pulled them on as he glanced at his bedside clock. Two thirty-six. His shirt had fallen to the floor but he could see it lying crumpled in the shadows. He pulled it on.

His front window faced the back of Laura's house, but he saw nothing amiss when he looked out. Nothing, that is, until the back screen door swung open and Laura slipped outside, down the porch stairs, and into the pouring rain.

He bolted outside and met her at the bottom of the stairs that led up to his apartment.

"Laura?" By instinct he kept his voice low. "What is it?"

Laura clutched his shirt front, heedless of the chilly rain which soaked her, though her whole body shivered. "Someone's in the house. Upstairs."

Justin glanced up at Elaine's bedroom window in time to see a light come on and filter through the closed blinds.

Laura tugged on his shirt trying to pull him toward the house. "Come on."

He shook his head. "Let's get you up to the apartment first, where it's warm and dry. My phone's up there, we'll need to call for help."

Laura let him support her up the stairs and into the apartment, where she sank into a corner chair. Justin grabbed his phone from the breakfast bar and automatically dialed Ed's number.

"Justin?" Ed always had a way of answering the phone sounding as if he'd been sitting right by it, waiting for it to ring, no matter the hour. A note of alarm tinged his greeting.

"Ed. There's an intruder in Laura's house."

"Where are you now?"

"In the garage apartment out back. Laura's with me."

"Stay there. We'll be along in a minute."

"Elaine's still in the house."

"Justin, you should stay with Laura."

"Ed—"

"OK, OK. We'll be right there."

Justin ended the call and handed the phone to Laura. "I'll be back in a bit."

Laura clutched the phone in both hands and looked suddenly frail and elderly. He paused to wrap an afghan around her shoulders and give her hands an encouraging squeeze. "It'll be OK. Ed's on his way and he'll bring help with him."

Then he bounded out the door, down the stairs and across the yard.

He eased the screen door open as quietly as possible and slipped inside. Voices came from upstairs—Elaine's and another muffled voice, male. He couldn't make out the words until Elaine raised her voice.

"Stop it, Junior!" she said, her tone strained with fear. "Stop it or I'll scream."

Silence.

Justin crept closer to the stairs, his right hand automatically reaching toward his hip for the service weapon that should have been there. The weapon that would have been there if not for the man upstairs terrorizing Elaine right now. In its absence he brought his hand up to his jaw and rubbed the stubble forming there.

Ed should be here any minute. Should he wait or go up? Was Junior armed? If so, with what? Was Junior alone, or had he brought an accomplice? The silence unnerved him. There was no way of telling what was happening. But no, he couldn't wait. Elaine needed him. He reached the front door and unbolted it, slowly, silently, then approached the stairs. He crept up one step then another.

"You think you won't get convicted for *this*!?" Elaine's voice carried down the stairs and Justin froze. "Aggravated sexual assault? Rape? Those carry heavier penalties than being drunk and disorderly, I can promise you. You'll be in prison for this for so long, nothing else you've done will even matter."

Aggravated sexual assault. He was armed. Did Elaine know he was there? Had she heard him downstairs? Had Junior heard him?

A real struggle began upstairs, now. Furniture scraped against the floor and wall. Glass shattered.

Then he heard a blow— either a punch or a slap, and Elaine cried out. The adrenaline induced rush turned to rage. He checked the urge to bound up the stairs. Best to go quietly. Junior was armed. He wasn't. His best bet was to catch him off guard. But Elaine...The struggle intensified as she fought, and the sound of more blows and more pain-stricken cries enraged him further.

"Stop it, Junior." she begged. "Please don't do this."

The words pierced like a knife in his heart. Up he went; two, three, four more steps, less mindful of the noise he made now.

"Justin!" He'd never heard so terrifying a scream.

Five, seven, nine. He took the stairs two at a time.

Silence again.

The struggle had stopped. Had Junior heard him coming? Justin froze, his breath caught in his chest. All he could hear was Junior's evil, nasal little laugh, then he murmured something indistinguishable in an equally vile tone.

"Oh, God, please no! Justin!" She screamed again. "Justin!"

He tore up the rest of the stairs and down the hall toward her room.

"Shut up!" Junior shouted.

Justin tried the knob, but the door was locked. He threw his shoulder into it once, twice, three times before the wood of the jamb splintered and gave way.

Junior sat straddling Elaine with one hand on her throat, choking her, and a gun pressed to her heart. Justin shouted his rage and launched himself across the room. A gunshot rang out. Then a hot, searing pain pierced his chest and exploded there, taking his breath.

He dropped to his knees.

He looked at Junior who had scrambled off the bed and backed up against the opposite wall, panic-stricken. The effort it took to shift his gaze to Elaine surprised him. Her face, equally as panic-stricken as Junior's, was swollen and discolored. Her lips were bloody, her nightgown torn.

"Elaine..."

A ringing began in his ears, its volume increasing steadily and swiftly. The pain in his chest vanished, as did the feeling in his arms and legs. He looked down to find his shirt front drenched in blood. But he just got a momentary glance before his vision faded to a pinpoint of light and he fell forward.

ҼҩҨ

She must have been out for a few seconds at most. Awareness came crashing back, relief at the ended attack colliding with even greater terror when she turned her head to see Justin on his knees with a bloodstain spreading rapidly over the front of his shirt.

"Elaine..." his voice sounded gravelly and his breathing shallow.

More footfalls approached, up the stairs and down the hall, coming closer.

He pressed both hands to the wound on his chest and looked down at it. Then he pitched forward and landed face down on the floor.

"Justin!" Elaine tried to call out, but her voice was gone. She swung her legs off the bed, but they buckled beneath her. So she crawled across the floor to where he lay face down in an expanding pool of blood.

Ed and Dale burst through the door with guns

drawn and shouts for Junior to drop his weapon and get down on the floor.

Elaine reached Justin and rolled him over onto his back. "No, no, no!" She cried, pushing the words over swelling vocal cords. She pressed her hands to Justin's wound to try to stop the blood. "Please, God, not again. Please!"

An image of Richard's lifeless body on a stretcher came unbidden as she recognized the signs of ebbing life in Justin. His face had drained of all color, he lay motionless and unresponsive. There was so much blood. How could he survive losing this much blood? "Please, God."

Dale was there with cloth to staunch the flow; he pressed it gently underneath her hands and held it there. He met her gaze silently.

"An ambulance..." she forced the hoarse words out.

"On its way." Dale said gently

"Justin." She whispered his name. "Please." Then she choked on a sob, silent only because she couldn't make a sound.

She was vaguely aware that Ed subdued and handcuffed Junior, hauled him up onto his feet and out of the room. But he was back a moment later, on his knees beside her, checking Justin for a pulse.

He searched, pressing his fingers into the flesh of Justin's throat, looking for the artery that would prove her worst nightmare had not truly come to pass a second time. At least, not yet. Ed's fingers stopped. His brow furrowed, then eased, and he nodded slowly.

Paramedics arrived with a gurney and took over for Dale, checking Justin's vital signs, then moving him onto the stretcher. Ed's arms lifted her off the floor, guiding her gently to the chair in the corner. Another paramedic waited to attend her as the gurney was wheeled out of the room.

She winced as her attendant gently prodded the wounds on her face, squinted as he shined a light in her eyes, checked her pulse, wrapped a blanket around her shoulders.

"Elaine," the paramedic's voice was soothing. "Did he rape you?"

She blinked and tried to clear her throat, trying to remember what had just happened. Junior had broken in, attacked her, but had he raped her? She shook her head. No. But the details were growing fuzzy already. He had pinned her down. She raised one hand to rub the bruised flesh of her wrist, then she lifted it to the spot on her chest where she could still feel the cold pressure of the gun muzzle. Then her hand moved to her throat as the realization dawned that he'd nearly choked the life out of her.

Hot tears welled in her eyes. The details were hazy, but they were there. Junior hadn't raped her. But he had shot Justin—maybe killed him.

"Try to remember, Elaine." Ed crouched in front of her. "We'll need to gather evidence."

Evidence. What was it about that word and the way Ed said it. *Evidence.* Always going on about the evidence and how he hadn't had enough to believe that Junior had been guilty of setting Justin up. She focused a cold stare at him. Maybe he had enough, now.

Her ears started ringing, and her gaze shifted as if on its own to the pool of blood on the floor beside her bed. Justin's blood.

"Justin..." She tried to say his name. Then shivers

began to rack her body. The chill came on unexpectedly, but a sweat broke out all over.

Another stretcher was wheeled in and she was helped onto it.

"Just lay back, Elaine." The paramedic murmured soothingly to her. Then he turned to his partner. "She's going into shock."

They got the stretcher downstairs and outside, and Ed took her hand as they wheeled her to a waiting ambulance. The shade of the night flashed blue then red in alternate turns as squad car lights pierced the darkness. She lifted her head to look around, but Justin was already gone.

Junior sat closed inside a squad car, his head resting against the window. He turned to look at her as they wheeled her past, locking eyes with her and sitting up to attention.

"I'm sorry!" he shouted through the closed door, his voice barely audible. "Elaine, I'm sorry! I never meant to—"

An officer stepped in front of the window, blocking her view.

"We'll all be praying, Elaine." Ed murmured to her, stroking her hand.

Tears stung and she closed her eyes as they lifted her stretcher into the back of the ambulance. "Please, God." She whispered as the doors closed. "Not again."

17

Elaine lay curled on her side, the crisp white hospital bedding pulled up to her chin. Shivers still racked her body, coming in violent waves then subsiding again, leaving her exhausted. They had given her a sedative and she had dropped off into dark oblivion for a time. Still she remained painfully aware of where she was, who had been to see her, who hadn't, and how much time had elapsed since Justin had crumpled lifelessly to her bedroom floor.

She was desperate to know how he was, and yet terrified to ask. No one brought it up. Not Ed or Dot. Not Aunt Laura. No one who had been to visit her in the last day had even uttered his name. There could only be one reason why.

"Please, God," Elaine whispered. "How will I survive this again?"

The door swung slowly open and Boyd Wendall came in, surveying her in that physician's way of his. He pulled a chair up next to her bed and sat down.

She squeezed her eyes shut and pressed her face into the pillow, using the tenderness of her flesh to immunize against the greater pain that was sure to come when he spoke.

Boyd's hand came gently to rest on her head and he stroked her hair. "Elaine?"

She opened her eyes and looked up at him,

knowing this was the moment he'd tell her Justin was dead, and her nightmares would begin all over again.

He took her hand in his. "Justin's in Austin."

Her heart lurched. Tears filled her eyes in a rush and began to fall freely. She rolled onto her back and tried to push up, but every muscle protested at the strain. "He's alive?"

Boyd blinked a few times. "Has no one told you?"

She sniffed and shook her head.

He let out a heavy sigh and handed her a tissue, then propped a pillow behind her back and head. He adjusted her bed so she could sit up. "Yes. Justin's alive." Boyd smiled, his tone was gentle. "He's critical. He's out of surgery, but we'll still have to wait and see what happens. He lost a lot of blood."

"When can I go?"

Boyd shook his head. "Not today."

"But—"

"Elaine, you've been beaten up, nearly raped. You have a bit of a concussion. You were in shock when you got here. I'd like you to stay until tomorrow."

"But...Justin—"

"Justin is where he needs to be. He's getting the best care possible. Vic and Lorraine are there with him. It won't help him any if you don't get better."

She opened her mouth to protest, but he held up his hand to silence her.

"Until tomorrow, Elaine. And only then if you can get someone else to drive you."

She relented and relaxed against her pillows with a nod.

"He'll be stronger by then. Maybe even conscious." He laid a steadying hand over hers, and she grasped at it, not realizing until this moment how hungry she was for a tender touch. "That was quite a thing he did." Boyd's voice was thick and soft.

Elaine closed her eyes, sending a new wash of tears down her cheeks as she nodded. A series of soft sobs shook her, as Boyd sat silently, holding her hand.

∂∽

The current pulled at him, purposefully determined to pull him under as he waded out to the stranded car. The woman inside yelled frantically, pleading for his help.

"Justin, we should wait!" Richard shouted from behind him. "The current's too fast!"

"Help me!" The stranded woman's screams tugged his attention back, further into the deadly torrent. *"Help my baby!"*

He glanced back at Richard. He was right. They couldn't stand against the current. He wasn't even knee deep and he was struggling to keep his footing.

"Help me!" Came the screams again, and when he turned back the current began taking her car with it, pushing it sideways, turning it around. If the current took it over the bridge she'd be in the creek, which had swollen into a river. He had to risk it.

He waded in deeper, less sure of his footing with each step he took. He was knee deep by the time he reached her car.

Her instinct was the same as his. She handed her baby out the window to him. The baby was actually about four years old and about forty pounds, but at least she could hold on, which she did for dear life, too scared to even cry.

Richard was wading toward him.

"Richard, go back!" He shouted over the sound of the pouring rain. "It's too strong!"

"No! You're right." Richard shouted back. "If we let her go off the bridge she'll never make it."

He thought he should argue, pull rank as a deputy sheriff to Richard's civilian status and order him back to solid ground. But exhaustion was already setting in. The muscles in his legs were quivering, his arms were cramping as much from the cold of the water as from its strong current, combined with the weight he carried. So he turned and headed back to dry ground.

Richard's cry for help came before he made it back. Justin pushed harder to get his burden to safety. It took just a half minute, at most. He crossed two or three other men headed into the deadly current as he reached dry ground. Someone took the child from his arms, and his knees nearly buckled from the suddenly reduced strain, but he stood his ground.

He turned around in time to see Richard losing his fight to stay on the bridge.

The current took him, but it was Elaine's voice he heard screaming his name.

"Justin!" She screamed as he plunged into sudden darkness. *"Justin!"*

Now he was in her bedroom watching as Junior sat straddled atop her, hitting her, over and over as she cried and struggled to defend herself.

"Justin!"

Junior pressed the muzzle of a handgun to her chest—to her heart.

And he couldn't move, couldn't speak. He was frozen to the spot, powerless once again to do anything but watch it happen.

Then the gun went off, but he knew it was his

heart that stopped.

❧❧

"Oh! My dear girl!" Mrs. Barnet rose and rushed across the room as Elaine entered. Ed and Aunt Laura were close behind her, keeping up with ease as the stiffness in her body slowed her down.

Justin's mother gently cupped Elaine's face in both her hands, the touch feather-light against her wounded flesh. Elaine had a first glimpse of her battered face this morning. The discolored and swollen image she'd seen in the mirror looked terrible. The tears in Mrs. Barnet's eyes now told the same story.

"I'm sorry." Elaine choked out the words. "This is all my fault."

"Oh, darlin', no!" Mrs. Barnet's arms came around her and she stroked Elaine's hair gently. "Shh. None of this is your fault." Lorraine took Elaine's hand in her own and led her to Justin's hospital bed.

She drew in a shocked breath at the sight of him. This man she had come to depend on looked so frail; weak and pale and small in comparison to his surroundings. As if he could just slip away at any moment. Tubes went everywhere, in his mouth and nose and arms. A respirator worked rhythmically beside his bed. Monitors clicked and beeped as he lay so quiet and still.

"Has he been awake at all, yet?" Her voice still sounded hoarse, though the thickness in her throat now was due to emotion.

Lorraine shook her head. "Not yet. But the nurses all say it should be any time now." She pressed Elaine gently into a chair facing his bed. "Talk to him, honey.

He needs to know you're all right."

She swallowed hard and touched his hand. It felt cool but pliable, and grateful tears sprang to her eyes and spilled over. Pliable and alive. Relief swelled.

"Justin." She whispered his name, linking her fingers through his. The door closed softly behind her and she sensed that the others had left them alone together. "I'm OK, baby. I'm here and I'm all right. I got out of the hospital today and I'm gonna be just fine." Another tear slid down her cheek. "You need to get better, too. So we can get married like we talked about. Justin, please...Please don't leave me." She laid her head down on the mattress beside him. "Please, Lord, don't take him from me. Not yet."

Those were all the words she remembered saying. Yet she remained there, beseeching God with her spirit, wordlessly asking Him to spare Justin. Her eyes drifted closed and she breathed in...out...in...out; in time to the respirator which kept him with her for now.

Please, Father. Her soul seemed to say.

He's mine. Came the reply. Not harsh, but insistent.

Yes, Lord.

She wouldn't argue. Justin had never been hers, just as Richard had never been, or their home and life together. Everything she had, God had given her, even the breath in her lungs right now. It was His to take.

You are mine. Not your own any longer.

Yes, Lord.

How easily it could have been her lying here, fighting for life. Junior hadn't intended to shoot anyone that night, she was pretty sure. But how easily his finger could have slipped on the trigger while he had the gun pressed to her heart, leaving her gone and Justin to grieve.

If I take him now, you will still be mine.

Yes, Lord. Always.

And if I take him now, how will you answer?

"Who am I to reply against You, God?" Elaine opened her eyes.

Justin lay there exactly as before, the monitors and machines still working, his chest still gently rising and falling. If God did take him now, she wouldn't go the same way she had before. She would stay and grieve, thanking God for the blessings rather than blaming Him.

She brought Justin's hand to her lips and pressed a kiss to it.

His arm twitched as if in reflex, a swift sudden little movement. Then he was with her again, awake and aware. His hand tightened around hers, and his eyelids fluttered open. He turned his head, searching for her, finding her.

He raised his hand to her face, brushing hair away from her swollen purple eye, running his thumb across the stitches on her cheekbone and the swollen scab covering her lower lip. Tears brimmed in his eyes and spilled. He couldn't talk for the tube running down his throat, but she knew what he wanted to say. That he loved her and he was sorry.

There wasn't much space on the mattress next to him, but she crawled gingerly onto it as his arm came around her. The hospital staff wouldn't approve, but for now they were alone.

"I love you, Justin."

His arm tightened around her in response.

She laid her head on his shoulder and took a deep breath. The strong steady beat of his heart pulled her pulse into the same rhythm. Her eyelids began to feel heavy. It wouldn't be long before she dropped off to sleep along side him.

There would be no better place than here, wrapped in the shelter of his arm, safe, secure and loved by a man who had been willing, quite literally, to die for her.

☙❧

The evening was waning and the sun would set within the hour. Elaine sighed heavily and rested her head on Justin's shoulder. They'd been sitting in the wicker double rocker on his mother's front porch for an hour. She had chatted about her day at work while he sat quietly, seeming to listen. But she wasn't sure he really heard a word she said. Boyd said this quietness of his, this withdrawal, was a normal part of his recovery, and time would settle it, just as time would settle her recent tendency to see demons and villains in every shadow. Post traumatic stress, that's what Boyd called it.

Now, however, she'd run out of things to say, so she sat quietly as Justin stroked the back of her hand with his.

"Ed came by to see me today." He spread his arm across the back of the rocker and she nestled beside him.

"To get your statement?"

He shook his head. "He got my statement awhile back."

"What did he want?" Elaine hadn't felt too kindly toward Ed in recent weeks. In her head, she knew no one but Junior was to blame for the attack on them. But part of her still wanted to hold Ed responsible. If he had believed in Justin's innocence he could have found the evidence he needed so badly to stop a lot of pain and suffering. Her attitude registered clearly in the tone of her voice, but she didn't try to mask it.

Justin's soft, warm kiss on her temple soothed her. *Forgive him.*

She took a deep breath, closed her eyes and forgave Ed again.

"He said Junior confessed."

Elaine couldn't stifle an ironic laugh. "Well, I imagine so, since he was caught with the smoking gun still in his filthy little hand."

"No, Elaine. He confessed."

She looked up at him. "You mean...?"

Justin nodded, a slow smile beginning.

Elaine pushed herself into an upright position and Justin winced at the sudden movement.

"Sorry." she added quickly, but his smile returned briefly, before it faded again.

"He did it while I was home."

"What?"

"While I was out back cutting the grass. The house was wide open. Junior snuck in through the garage, hid the drugs and left."

"But what about the bag with your fingerprints?"

"He took it from the garbage weeks before."

Junior was either way smarter than she had ever given him credit for, or way more stupid. "What else did Ed say?"

"He said that, in light of the new *evidence,* there shouldn't be any trouble getting a judge to overturn my conviction."

Her breath caught. "Oh, Justin!" A fresh batch of tears stung her eyes. Having his conviction overturned would mean so much. A judge would officially declare him innocent. The real culprit would finally take the blame and punishment for everyone to see. His name and reputation would be restored.

He held up a hand to stay her enthusiasm and she clutched it, intertwining her fingers with his.

"He also said that as soon as that happened, and as soon as I'm up to it, I can be reinstated as a deputy."

She clamped a hand over her mouth to hold back a joyful sob. *Finally!* Justice.

Justin's grin turned into a full smile. "He *also* said that a settlement from the state would probably be in order and he would be the first to testify on my behalf if necessary."

She dropped her hand, eyes wide. "A settlement?" She breathed the word.

"Three years worth of lost wages and benefits, plus the pain and suffering of being falsely imprisoned...It could amount to a nice little sum. Enough to buy a house for us." He paused and pulled her to him. "Or fix up an old one. Or build a completely new one."

"Oh, Justin." she sighed and wrapped her arms around him. "I'd live in that old trailer out back. As long as we can be together."

He tipped her chin up so she was looking into his eyes.

"I love you, Elaine."

"I love—" He pressed his fingers to her lips, cutting off her automatic reply.

"I tried..." His voice grew suddenly thick and he paused. "I could hear you screaming for me upstairs. I knew Junior was armed, but I hesitated. I thought for a minute I should wait for Ed." He traced the scar on her cheek with a gentle finger. "But if I had just gotten there sooner none of this might have happened.

"I tried so hard. I couldn't save Richard, and I couldn't protect you either—"

"Couldn't protect me...?" She echoed his words, not understanding. "But you did. Junior didn't rape me, but he would have if you hadn't come in when you did." She shuddered. The bruises on her knees where he'd tried so violently to shove them apart weren't painful anymore, but she could still feel the blows that put them there. "He might have killed me." She ended in a whisper and a hard swallow, still able to feel the constriction of Junior's hand on her throat.

"And when I think how easily his finger could have twitched on the trigger when he had that gun..." Her voice trailed off and she pressed her hand to her heart.

Justin covered her hand with his and kissed her softly.

"But he shot you instead, and you..." Her voice failed as an image of him on his knees, blood spreading rapidly on his shirt front, came unwanted. She squeezed her eyes shut and willed it away.

"I'm the one who could have prevented all this. If I just hadn't provoked him in the first place. Or if I hadn't struggled so hard. If I'd just told him what he wanted me to say. If I'd just...just let him..." The revulsion of the thought took her breath.

Justin shook his head.

But she continued. "If I'd just..." She laid her hand lightly on his chest, over his gunshot wound. "I was so stupid, Justin. I knew he had a gun, and I still fought and screamed, and made him madder and madder. And then he shot you, and I thought you were dead...For a whole day I thought—" Her voice failed before she could finish.

He wrapped both arms around her and held on.

"But I'm not." He whispered against her hair. "And neither are you."

Dusk was coming on the early summer breeze, the bright blue of the cloudless evening sky turning lavender-gray and pink, and fiery at once. Just a few yards away a lone cotton tail hopped across the gravel drive into a tall patch of grass. On a sigh, Elaine let the memories of that night disappear with it as she relaxed in Justin's arms.

"I wonder how things might have been different if I hadn't run off after the tornado."

Justin pressed a kiss to the top of her head. "Everything's all right, now. That's all that matters. And tomorrow's a new day."

"But if I had stayed—"

"Shh. It's all right, now. Let's just go from here."

They sat in silence for awhile. Long enough that her eyelids began to feel heavy as the rocking of the chair they were in began to lull her to sleep.

"So," Justin's low, rich-timbred voice stirred her. "Would you like quartz counter tops in your new kitchen, or would you prefer granite?"

She smiled.

Would she always remember this feeling? One day they'd be married and arguing over some little thing, like quartz or granite counter tops, or where to go for dinner or on vacation. Or maybe they'd be fighting about something big, like money or children. She nestled herself a little more snugly into the crook of his arm with a secret smile, praying that in those moments God would remind her of this moment; when she felt blessed to be alive and unharmed beside Justin, when things could have ended so differently.

Please, God, she prayed, asking Him to not let this moment fade from her memory; this moment when she felt peace beyond measure.